One Night in a Thousand Years

by Craig Cunningham

Published by Canowan Books

CANOWAN

ISBN 979-8-218-09813-1

For Jonathan and the Warrior Poets

Prologue

The field is no longer empty. Now it's lined with gray stones.

A decade later the air still smells the same. The tunnel of oak trees provides the same patchwork shade. Everything is just like it used to be.

Except for the field.

Back then, when I first came here with Lucas, he said, "One day we'll come to this spot and it will be covered in tombstones. Every plot will be sold and filled. You or I could be buried here. Maybe we'll get another fifty years. Or, maybe just another week."

He was right.

The only thing that has changed at Oakwood Cemetery are the amount of people in the ground. What was once the promise of more time — the field — has been transformed into a reminder that time eventually runs out for all of us.

Time.

The greatest mystery of all. And it never stops moving, but sometimes it slows down so we can pause and take in the absolute beauty of life.

Time slowed down when I was a senior in high school.

Time slowed down in the sacred circle.

Time slowed down the first night I kissed her.

I wove through the tombstones looking for the name. Eventually I found him.

My heart thudded faster. All of a sudden, I was seventeen again. I stood in a circle around a campfire. I saw their faces in the flickering light. This wasn't just nostalgia. This was something far more powerful. I remembered all of the reasons to be alive.

"I came home. Just like I promised," I said.

I bent down before the gravestone and ran my fingers over the name. I knew he wasn't here. He had never been here. There was no body in the ground beneath me. Just an idea. Maybe he was always just an idea.

"I've missed you, old friend. We've all missed you."

The wind picked up, and for the first time I noticed the oak tree that had grown behind the tombstone. The leaves shuddered in the early October chill. I remembered planting that acorn a decade earlier, just before leaving.

Nothing happens by accident.

Not an asteroid hitting the earth.

Not a first kiss.

Not a stranger who destroys your life.

Let me go back . . .

One Night in a Thousand Years

Craig Cunningham

1

I stood in front of the main entrance, not sure if I had the inner strength to take another step forward.

The great, evil mothership called high school was sprawled out before me.

Senior year. Woo-hoo.

I entered the front doors and worked my way through a line of nervous freshmen picking up their schedules. There was always a buzz on the first day of school, like maybe this was the year when everything would come together. Maybe this was the year when you get the girl or make the grades or play the hero. Then reality hits, and it turns out that you're the same person you've always been.

I heard a shout.

"Colt!"

James Ray wrapped his burly arm around my neck.

"Bro! Where were you last night?"

"What?"

"The party. On Maddie's houseboat. I told you about it."

"Oh right. I totally forgot."

"You're riding with me from now on. I'm sick of you missing out."

Truthfully, I hadn't forgotten about it. I just didn't want to go.

A few weeks earlier I was driving home half-drunk from a party when I swerved and crashed through the median and slid into the opposite side of the highway. Thank God nobody was coming. It was so late that the roads were clear for as far as I could see. I got out of my truck and checked both ways. It felt like I was all alone in the world, or like I'd entered some kind of parallel universe. No headlights could be seen coming from either direction. I climbed on top of the cab and noticed the stars spread thick above me. The stars. All these years and I'd never truly paused to look up and realize how beautiful they were, but in that moment I couldn't look away. Eventually, headlights came over the distant horizon so I got in the truck and drove home like nothing happened, like everything was fine.

I never told anyone.

But something inside of me changed after that night. What if it all came to an end *like that*? What if someone had been coming, right at that moment? What if they had a family? What if the family was in the car with them?

The thoughts ate me up.

The stars ate me up.

"Katz puked in someone's mailbox on the way home," James said. "It was epic. We were just swimming around the marina, fishing, whatever. It was fun. But I'm not the same without my wingman."

"Yeah, I'll be there next time."

"I know you will. Because I'm going to make sure of it."

James guided me down the center of the hallway as if the whole school were his personal kingdom. We'd been best friends ever since elementary school when his family moved into the house next to ours. Every summer, we built treehouses and raced bikes and roamed the neighborhood. This summer, he spent a night in juvie for tipping over port-a-potties at the county fair. Some lady was inside of one and made a big scene. Standing at six foot three, James made an impression on every room he entered, not only with his mammoth frame but also the caveman energy that made him the most popular guy in school, even though plenty of people hated his guts.

Up ahead, Coach Julip walked toward us. He wore a pair of red spandex shorts that stopped halfway up his thighs and revealed way more than we wanted to see. He pointed at me as he passed by.

"You focused? Ready for Friday?"

"I am, Coach."

"Stay that way. Don't let yourself get . . . distracted," he said, eyeing James.

"I'll be ready."

After he passed us, James scoffed. "Can you believe that guy? Did you see the way he looked at me? He's trying to own your life, bro. And you're *letting him*. You're letting him. You gotta get control of yourself and realize what it means to be a senior. Watch. Perfect example."

James motioned at two pretty freshmen girls walking side by side in front of us. He sped up and split them down the middle, putting his arms around their shoulders.

"Good morning, ladies. My name is James, and I want to personally welcome you to your first day of high school. And if you ever need anything, and I mean anything, you just let me know. Or let Colt know. That's Colt," he said, motioning back at me. "He's the captain of the football team. So if you ever want to come to a senior party, or get a private tour of the school, we will be at your service. Because we so, so, so badly want to get to know you."

They sheepishly escaped his grip and entered a classroom. He whistled at them, waving off their teacher who gave him a look of death.

"Colt . . . this is everything we've ever wanted." James pulled me close. "We're here, man. We're gods for a year. And I love it."

Principal Villarreal leaned against the stairwell up ahead. On seeing me and James, he stepped forward, twirling his lanyard around his finger. Villarreal was the kind of guy who carried a comb in his front pocket and slicked his hair back in the middle of a conversation. He was hardcore about the dress code and was honestly one of the most confrontational people I'd ever met. We always figured a day would come when he would totally lose it on some kid.

James gave him a big phony smile and hollered, "Well, hey there sir!"

"Boys . . ." Villareal said. "New year, new attitudes, new responsibilities. Right?"

"You took the words right out of my mouth, sir!"

"Good to hear. The freshmen are looking up to you. Remember that. Watching your every move. We need some *bona fide* leaders in this school. I can't do it all on my own."

"Oh, I don't doubt that, sir," James said.

Villarreal got in James's face.

"You got something you want to say to me?"

"Just that I agree you can't do it on your own."

"What do you say I walk you to class? Just so I'll know

where to find you."

"That'd be an honor, sir. A real honor." James winked at me. "We'll catch up later, bro. Remember. Gods for a year."

Villarreal hovered beside him as they turned down another hallway.

If this kept up, it was going to be a long year.

I checked my schedule one more time and went to Room 232. English Lit.

Nobody else was in the classroom when I arrived. Even the teacher was gone. She had placed a paperback book on the center of every desk, so I randomly picked a seat and sat down.

The book was called *Essays* by Ralph Waldo Emerson.

I thumbed through the book and noticed the pages were covered in handwriting. We were all used to having hand-me-down books, but this one felt particularly beat up, like it should have been recycled a long time ago. I started reading through the handwritten notes on the pages . . .

"Hey Colt."

I glanced up. Noa sat in front of me. She was turned around in her seat and staring at me.

"Oh. Hey."

"You alright? You were pretty zoned out, there."

"Yeah, sorry. I was just reading ahead . . . how was summer?"

I closed the book.

Noa.

It was good to have a friend in class. And I was happier to see her than I expected. Honestly, the feeling caught me off guard. We'd been close for a while, even though she ran with a different crowd. She wore her hair up in a messy bun and had a pair of clear plastic eyeglasses, which I didn't remember from junior year. A few summer freckles were spread across her nose and cheeks. But the main thing you noticed looking at Noa were her bright green eyes.

"It was good. I worked at the froyo shop. Making *all kinds* of minimum wage. Learned to play a few new tunes from Thelonious Monk. Went on a trip to Nairobi."

"Oh wow. Remind me where that is?"

"Kenya. In Africa."

"For vacation?"

"No, with Habitat for Humanity. We built an orphanage for kids who are HIV positive. It was a pretty amazing experience. What'd you do?"

Let's see . . . almost died in a drunk driving accident . . . screwed around town . . .

"Just hung out with friends, mostly. Nothing big."

"What's with your book?"

"Huh?"

"You were super focused when I came in."

She motioned down at my copy of Emerson's *Essays*.

"Oh. Somebody wrote notes all over the pages. I was trying to see what they say."

"Anything juicy?"

She playfully raised her eyebrows at me.

"Not sure. But I'll let you know if I find anything."

I had no way of knowing then.

But the person who wrote those notes was coming to ruin my life.

2

I sat in the football locker room, head down, still dripping wet from the shower.

Everybody else had already left and one of the trainers was turning out the lights one by one.

"You alright, Colt?"

I nodded.

"Yeah. Give me five minutes."

He wheeled the cart of dirty uniforms toward the laundry room.

When you give up a three-touchdown lead in the fourth quarter, you start asking questions about who was responsible. Tonight, it was me. Maybe you could call it a lack of focus. Maybe you could call it bad luck. But it was me.

"Lights are going out, Colt. I need to lock up . . ."

The lights went out. I got dressed in the pitch black and felt my way to the door.

When I stepped out into the night, James was pacing under the awning of the entrance. He threw his hands up when he saw me.

"Finally. There you are. You ready?" he asked.

"For what?"

"For the best night of our lives."

"I want to go home and forget about tonight."

Saying yes to James meant opening yourself up to absolute chaos. He pinned me against the brick wall.

"Colt, I'm going to say this one more time. We are seniors. You are the captain of the football team. It is Friday night. And I'll be damned if I let you go home and crawl in your little bed-dy-bed and fall asleep. No more excuses."

"James . . . "

He hooted so he couldn't hear my refusal. My back was sore, and the last thing I felt like doing was getting caught up in a late night.

James draped his arm over my neck and led me toward the parking lot where a pack of guys had piled into three trucks. They banged on the side paneling when they saw me. One of them threw me a football, and I tossed it back. Bill Scott blew a trumpet. He had stolen it from a band kid.

"Captain Colt has arrived!" James called out. "Let's roll, boys!"

I jumped into the bed of the truck next to James and held on as we sped out of the parking lot and onto the main drag.

"Where are we going?" I asked.

"You'll see," James said. He ripped a swig from a flask of whiskey. "We'll be legends. Everyone will be talking about this on Monday."

The two other trucks followed behind us, packed to the brim. I rode along, the early September wind in my face, not knowing the decision to ride with them would change my entire senior year. If I had known what was going to happen, I never would have gone. But if I had never gone, nothing would have changed.

And I needed change.

We wove around the post-game traffic and soon turned into a neighborhood of nice houses. The three trucks cut the lights, and everyone fell silent as we rolled to a stop. I saw the target house. In the front yard was a ten-foot-tall inflatable panther, the school mascot.

"Who lives here?"

"Our best buddy," James said with a playful grimace. "Villarreal."

As in, *Principal* Villarreal. I should have seen it coming. The two of them had been on a collision course ever since junior year when James put photos of Villarreal's face on the bodies of swimsuit models and taped them to random lockers throughout the school. Villarreal lost his mind and said James was standing in front of 'a freight train of pain'. And now here we were outside his house.

Everyone hopped out. They seemed to already have a plan, so I stood with my hands in my pockets watching. One group unloaded a yellow speed bump from a truck. Miles waddled a bucket of fresh cement toward Villarreal's driveway. He spread the paste thick on the ground while they arranged the speed bump on top. I had to give them credit for creativity.

The porch light flipped on.

"*Mayday! Mayday!*" James shouted. He jumped into the driver's seat of our truck and turned the ignition. "Let's go!"

I ran with the others and grabbed onto the edge of the truck. But I couldn't swing my other leg inside before James put the pedal to the metal. As the truck spun onto the next street, I flung off and smashed my ankle against the curb. Pain shot up my leg. The three trucks cruised into the night and disappeared around the bend.

I must have blacked out for a minute, because when I woke up Villarreal was standing over me.

He took out a comb and ran it through his hair.

"You're finished, Colt. You're toast, and it's breakfast time."

3

The second I entered the front doors of the school on Monday morning, Villarreal was waiting for me. He snickered at my crutches and the boot on my foot.

"Hey there, Colt. Hopping around okay?"

"I'm fine."

"You and me are going to spend some quality time together today. Let's go."

Villarreal led me to his office, where Coach Julip paced around in his red spandex shorts.

"What the hell did you do, Colt?"

"I didn't do anything."

I plopped into the leather chair next to Coach and leaned my crutches against the wall.

"What did the doctor say?"

"It's broken in two places."

Coach Julip removed his ball cap and scratched his forehead with a grimace.

"You are an absolute squirrel turd," Villarreal said, taking a seat behind his desk. "I should paddle you on the morning video announcements for everyone to see. You know I have that authority."

"I had nothing to do with it. I swear. I came out of the locker room and got in a truck and that's where the trucks went."

"You think it's funny to install a speed bump in my driveway? You think it's funny to draw weenies on my inflatable panther?"

"I mean, sort of . . . but that doesn't mean I think it was a good idea."

"Are you trying to provoke me, mister hot shot?"

"No sir."

Coach Julip slid a piece of paper in front of me.

"Write down everybody's name that was there."

Villarreal tossed me a pen.

"Every name. First and last."

I glanced over my shoulder to meet eyes with Noa through the windows that looked out into the commons. She motioned at my foot and asked if I was okay. I shook my head no.

"Hey. Hey. Don't mess with a sweet girl like her," Villarreal said. "She's on the Honor Roll, and you're *this close* to being on the Get-Kicked-Out-Of-School Roll."

"I can't write down the names."

"If you don't, it's all coming down on you. I know James was there. And Katz. Sam. Lamar. Who else?"

"I don't remember."

"What's wrong with you?" Julip asked. "Are you concussed?"

"No. I'm feeling fine."

Even though they left me in the street with a broken ankle, I couldn't rat them out like a coward.

"Let me paint a picture for you," Villarreal said softly. He took an ancient wooden paddle out from a drawer in his desk.

"In an instant, everything you love is taken away from you. Your friends. Your freedom. Your family. Your future. And you're all alone, begging for help. And when you look up, no one is there to save you. But you hear footsteps." He tapped the paddle on the desk to imitate footsteps. "You get a burst of hope. *Oh, maybe my precious little senior year can be saved. Maybe I won't be a total loser.* But when those footsteps arrive you realize it's me, holding this paddle coming to whoop your rear end and send you back to the hell you've created for yourself. Now . . . give me the names."

"I'm not giving you any names."

He flung the paddle against the wall in an attempt to scare me straight. Seeing I wasn't going to budge, he reached for the telephone on his desk and dialed a number.

"Yes," he said into the phone. "This is Principal Villarreal. Just letting you know that I'm sending a student your way for a few weeks. He'll be hopping along shortly."

*

That evening I told my parents the punishment.

ISS, which meant I'd be sitting in a windowless storage unit for six weeks with a few psychopaths and a retired gym teacher. I figured if I put my head down and suffered through it, I'd be fine. Anything was better than being a coward and bending the knee to Villarreal. My parents already knew what happened. When your ankle swells up to the size of a beach ball and turns black, your parents are going to notice. Dad took me to the ER late Friday night and I had confessed the whole story.

But my official punishment gave them a brand-new opportunity to share life lessons about my friends, my choices, my integrity, my you-name-it. I finally convinced them I needed to get started on homework.

Senior year. Woo-hoo.

I went to my bedroom and unloaded my backpack onto my desk.

The Emerson book fell open onto the floor. I saw the notes written in the margins and bent down to pick it up. I flipped through a few pages and stopped at one of the many passages that had been underlined:

If the stars should appear one night in a thousand years, how would men believe and adore; and preserve for many generations the remembrance of the city of God which had been shown! But every night come out these envoys of beauty, and light the universe with their admonishing smile.

The stars. I thought back to that night on the highway.

I scanned more pages. Every inch of the margins was filled with notes in the same handwriting. But not just normal notes. It was almost like someone's personal journal, their every thought about the book. Their every thought about life, really.

Part of me felt like I was intruding on someone's privacy, but another part of me felt this overwhelming, unexplainable sense that the messages were written for me.

So I kept on reading.

. . . I was not made to serve someone else's dreams for my life . . .

. . . Destiny requires sacrifice . . .

. . . If you love her, you must leave her . . .

. . . How long will you carry the shame?

. . . Yesterday does not exist. Tomorrow does not exist. Only today . . .

I flinched at a knock on my bedroom door.

"Colt, you have a visitor," Dad called.

Maybe James had finally come to apologize for leaving me to take the heat. It was about time. I put on a shirt and walked out to the entryway where Noa stood carrying a smoothie and a folder. Mom and her were talking and laughing about something.

"Oh. Hey Noa."

"Hey."

"Well, it was good to catch up," Mom said. "Hope I'll be seeing you soon."

She winked as she walked past me.

"Sorry if she was . . . nosy or anything," I said quietly to Noa.

"Your assignments."

Noa handed me the folder. She was wearing workout clothes and the edge of her hair was still damp with sweat.

"Right. Thanks."

"And a smoothie for you. Because aren't smoothies supposed to heal broken ankles?"

I smiled. "Thanks. Yeah, I've heard that."

There was an awkward pause.

"Well, I hope you start feeling better," she said, turning toward the door.

"Wait. You want to stay for a minute?"

She checked her phone for the time and gave me a smile.

"I should go. My parents are expecting me home," she said. "Get better, okay?"

"Okay. Thanks for the smoothie."

"Also, I know you're pretty busy, or whatever, but I'm going to this youth group thing on Sunday night if you want to come. It should be fun. We could even ride together, if you wanted. Anyways, no pressure."

"Oh. Yeah. I'm kind of grounded so we'll see. And I'll probably have a lot of school to catch up on."

"Right. No pressure. Just an idea if you wanted to . . . nevermind. Have fun with Emerson."

She smiled at me, then headed out the front door. As soon as the door closed, my mom stepped into the room and threw a kitchen towel at me.

"Are you stupid?" she asked.

"What?"

"Colt . . . you're going with her on Sunday. She's precious."

4

So, look.

My mom was right. But she was also very wrong. Yes, I wanted to spend more time with Noa, and my mom obviously liked that she was interested in me. She had never been particularly impressed with my other girlfriends. That part was all well and good.

But I also had a decent understanding of how these Sunday night church services happened to go. Church wasn't really my thing. I didn't have anything against people who went. Most of them seemed nice enough. What I couldn't get past was the way the leaders tried to manipulate everyone's emotions and make you think the same way as them.

For example, back in middle school I went to a church summer camp. One night the pastor gathered all of the boys together and took out a hammer and some nails. He gave his sermon about how disappointing we were to God, then hammered nails into a board. With every strike of the hammer he claimed each one of our sins was another nail going into the hands and feet of Jesus, and we'd better repent or else we'd go to hell, and all that.

Everybody either left in tears or was terrified into conversion.

But after a week of ISS, I would have accepted an invitation to dig a ditch.

So on Sunday night, I found myself following Noa up to the second floor of the church and walked into the youth room.

Gideon, the youth pastor, stood on stage. The lights were down and the audience was fuller than I expected, all high school students. Noa found us a pair of empty seats.

On stage, Gideon gave instructions about how the groups of students would be split up by grade and gender for the rest of the school year, and how every group had a designated classroom in the church. Gideon seemed like a decent enough guy. He read off a list of college-age leaders, room numbers, and who went where. The purpose of these small groups was for teenagers to be mentored by college kids from the nearby university, and for us to grow spiritually over the course of the school year. He said we'd be 'sharpening' one another.

The lights came up and Noa squeezed my arm.

"Ugh, I'm so excited," she said. "Our leader is super cool. She runs this nonprofit that helps women transition out of the sex industry. I seriously can't believe she's leading a group."

"I'm with someone named Lucas Oliver. The name sounds familiar, but I can't figure out why."

Noa's eyes widened.

"Yeah . . ."

"What?"

"I don't personally know him. But I've heard he's sort of . . . strange."

"Like, how?"

"Like, he's far out there. In his own world."

She took off to meet her leader, leaving me standing there

alone and wishing I was anywhere else.

A few other senior guys huddled toward the hallway. I already recognized most of them from school, so I walked over.

"I didn't expect to see you here," Charlie said, bumping my fist.

"I didn't really expect to be here," I confessed.

Charlie was sort of a jokester, beloved by all groups and allegiant to none.

Then came Amado and Malik. They competed in high-level science fairs around the state and ran semi-illegal experiments in the shed behind Malik's house. They mostly followed their own interests and kept distance from everyone else.

Next up was Ortiz. He stood at six feet four inches tall and ran track and field. Ortiz built websites for companies and made a grown man's salary, which he supposedly invested in the stock market.

Finally, as expected, came Peter Dietrich, a purebred church boy with a mother who dressed like a pioneer. He didn't go to our school because she ran a homeschool operation.

This was the crew that would be sharpening one another.

We found our classroom down the hall, but no one was there. I figured maybe Lucas was in the bathroom or just running late. But when I looked around, I noticed something written on the green chalkboard on the far wall. It read:

"Where everyone thinks alike, no one is thinking."

<u>Meet me in the parking lot behind the church.</u>

We glanced around at each other, confused. Then we took the staircase down and out of the church to the back parking lot.

A barrel fire burned in the far corner of the parking lot and a beat-up old pickup truck was backed up next to it. The guy warming his hands over the flames was about five or ten years older than me, with long hair and a beard. We all figured this must be Lucas Oliver.

"Hey guys. Pull your cars around here," he said as we got close. "Back them in to make a circle."

We backed our vehicles into a circle and settled on truck beds, bumpers, and lawn chairs around the fire.

Then, something strange happened.

We just sat there in total, absolute silence.

Lucas stared at us, like he was waiting on one of us to step forward and lead the group. Like he was curious what we were going to do. When the awkwardness reached its peak, Peter handed him the printout of the weekly curriculum. Lucas balled up the paper and threw it into the fire. It felt like an eternity passed before he stood off his tailgate and approached the fire. I didn't know what exactly was going on, but I knew this wasn't how church groups were supposed to go.

Lucas looked up at the stars and took a big breath of the night sky.

"When I was seventeen, the last thing I wanted to do was sit in a room and listen to someone tell me what to think about God and about life. I had questions, dreams, ideas, as I know each of you here tonight do. And so our time together this year is going to be about you figuring out who you are, what you believe, and who you want to be." He paused, then continued, "A year from this very moment, each of you will be off on your own. And if you haven't examined the perspective that's been handed to you up to this point, then you'll simply be regurgitating what others have told you to think and to be. That said, our journey isn't going to be about me teaching you answers. It's going to be about you asking the questions that start you on a worthy journey. It's about finding your true heart."

Lucas opened the passenger seat of his truck and took out a stack of leather journals. He tossed one to each of us.

Everything in me wanted to toss it back. To say no thanks. To reject another person's attempt to guide me into their way of thinking. But this felt *different*. Lucas didn't seem interested in that sort of thing. He seemed . . . real.

"Consider tonight an invitation," he said. "Ask yourself if you're willing to enter the mystery. If you are, I'll see you here in this same spot next week."

Without another word, Lucas climbed into his truck and drove away.

We sat in stunned silence for a minute before Peter asked, "Does anybody know what just happened?"

In a way, I did. This all sounded eerily familiar.

When I got home that night, I picked up the Emerson book and quickly turned to the last page that listed the previous students who had been assigned the book before me.

There it was. The name written in the same handwriting as all the notes in the margins.

Lucas Oliver.

Nothing happens by accident.

Nothing.

5

They let me out of ISS to have lunch with all the normal kids, but I wanted fresh air. The ISS room didn't have windows and I was starting to feel like a sardine. I went outside with a sack lunch and sat on my tailgate to eat in peace.

Since the accident I hadn't heard a word from James or any of the other guys. They left me out to dry. To make matters worse, someone finished the job and installed a series of speed bumps in Villarreal's driveway and stuck the inflatable panther with a screwdriver. It sounded like a copycat job but he interrogated me again and threatened to 'whoop my tooshie' on the morning video announcements.

Halfway through my sandwich I looked across the parking lot to see Wayne Derrick eating on his tailgate. I packed up everything and walked over to him. Wayne and school were like oil and water. He nearly flunked every year, and none of his teachers expected him to amount to much in life.

"Hey Wayne. What's going on?"

"Not a lot. Just thinking to myself that I don't understand why the state legislature thinks we need twelve whole years of this. School, I mean."

"Well, this is our last year."

"Don't jinx me," he said.

He was listening to the local Mexican radio station.

"You speak Spanish?" I asked.

"Not yet. But I like the way it sounds. It's just *boom boom boom* one word after another without a breath. It's erotic."

"Mind if I take a seat?"

"Go for it."

I sat on the tailgate of his early '90s 4Runner. In the back he had a gas can and some replacement wires for a weed-eater.

"I heard you got busted for screwing with Villarreal," Wayne said.

"Yeah. But I didn't do anything."

"I heard that too. Sucks about your ankle."

"Yeah. It's all right."

"Those guys are jerks, man. No offense. I know they're your friends and all. But one day they'll get what's coming. You didn't deserve all that."

I ate my sandwich.

"I didn't mean to offend you," he added.

"You didn't. You're right."

He drank coffee from a big travel mug like a long-haul trucker.

"You remember what James did to me? I haven't forgotten about it."

I nodded. A couple of years ago James told everyone he saw Wayne naked and that his dick was royal blue. Wayne did his best to dispel the rumor. The joke stood the test of time even if no one believed it.

"Yeah. He's like that."

"Why are you friends with him then?"

I wished I could explain, but friendship turns complicated as you get older. As kids, me and James spent more time together in the summers than we spent apart. He always acted like a skid mark, but no one ever heard the conversations we had about the places we wanted to go when we grew up or about how he wished his dad didn't travel so much for work. Those kinds of conversations dried up over the years. Now, most of his energy was spent convincing college guys to buy him beer.

"I've been asking myself the same question lately. I've been asking lots of questions lately," I said to Wayne.

"Like what?"

"Nothing. It's stupid. Just about life."

He offered the coffee to me.

"No thanks. Hey, this may sound kind of weird, but there's a group of guys getting together on Sunday night in the church parking lot at seven. You should come."

"At the church? I dunno." His mind hunted for an excuse. "I have a pretty busy schedule."

"Yeah, no pressure. But you're welcome."

The bell rang and a police officer patrolling the parking lot motioned for us to go inside. We tossed our trash into a bin and walked to the entrance. Inside, Wayne stopped me.

"What's the question? The one you've been asking."

I checked over both shoulders to make sure no one was paying attention. I don't know why I felt embarrassed to say it aloud.

"Just . . . trying to figure out the point of all this. Asking why we're here."

He nodded in understanding and put a hand on my shoulder.

"It's the state legislature, man. They have to be dismantled. Twelve years of this stuff is simply too long."

6

Maybe I would have ignored Lucas's invitation were it not for the book. What were the odds that I would sit at that desk, pick up *that* book, and then randomly meet the guy who wrote those words almost a decade earlier?

The universe seemed to be speaking directly to me, and, for the first time, I intended to listen.

The next Sunday night, there was no barrel fire in the far corner of the church parking lot. But we could see Lucas's truck backed up next to another car I recognized to be Wayne's. I guess his busy schedule opened up.

"You all can jump in the back of my truck," Lucas said as we approached him. "I want to show you something."

"Where are we going?" Peter asked.

"It's not far."

"Does Gideon know we're leaving? Should I call my mom?"

Lucas cranked the window up and started the truck.

We reluctantly climbed into his rusted truck bed. Wayne nudged me with his elbow as if to say hello.

"Is this legal?" Peter whispered. "There's no seatbelts. Where are we going?"

"Chill, Peter."

The truck rolled forward, and we hunkered down as he merged onto the highway.

A few minutes later, we turned into Oakwood Cemetery, a pretty place with a main road shadowed by a tunnel of century-old oak trees. The graves popped out of the ground for as far as I could see in every direction. Some of the prominent families were buried in striking mausoleums, guarded by sword-carrying angels. The truck wound toward the back of the cemetery.

Questions rolled through my mind, the main one being: *What the hell are we doing in the cemetery at night?*

Based on the looks of the other guys' faces, I could tell they were wondering the same.

Lucas finally parked in the middle of the graveyard beneath a canopy of oaks. Twilight blanketed the tombs, and the last fireflies of summer floated around us. He stepped in front of the truck as we gathered around him, waiting to see what this field trip was all about.

"Each of these gravestones tells a story. Of greatness, or of regret. Each warns us that life is more precious than we can possibly imagine. How many of these people lived out the potential that was within them? How many settled for mediocrity?"

He took out a pipe and stuffed it full of tobacco, then struck a match and huffed it to life.

"Tonight, I'd like each of you to take twenty minutes and walk through the graves. Alone. Silent. Think of what each person's life might have been like. What they dreamed, what they gave their hearts to, and what they regretted. Listen to what the dead have to teach us," he said.

Lucas turned and strolled off into the coming darkness.

I could sense most of the guys were uncomfortable with the proposition of walking around a graveyard at night and wanted to go back to the church. But we each stepped out into the maze of graves and went our own way.

I found myself reading the dates on the tombstones. Sure, some of the people lived long lives. But others died young. *Too young.* Did the seven-year-old get sick? Was the eighteen-year-old in some kind of accident? Their names and dates revealed incomplete stories. I wanted to know what their lives would have been like if they had lived. Even though it was growing darker by the minute, I found myself wandering further and further into the cemetery, lost in a sea of half-lived stories. And even the ones who lived to old age . . . did they make the most of their time? Or did they just kind of float along until the end?

None of them knew when they were going to die. They woke up one morning and didn't make it to the next one.

Lucas whistled. It was the signal for us to meet back up. Twenty minutes vanished.

I caught my breath. I felt something strange fluttering inside of me. An urgency to live.

I made my way back in the darkness and found the guys staring out over an empty field at the back of the graveyard.

"It's haunting, isn't it?" Lucas said.

"What is?" Charlie asked.

"All the empty space. People living and breathing on the planet alongside us right now in this very moment will be buried here someday. One day we'll come back to this spot and it will be covered in tombstones. Every plot will be sold and filled. You or I could be buried there. Maybe we'll get another fifty years. Or, maybe just another week."

The thought sent a chill up my spine. If the graves taught me anything, it was that someone in our group might die before their time. Like Lucas said, it could be any of us. Even me.

"Alright, let's head back before Gideon wonders where we went."

We didn't say much on the ride back to the church. The sticky, hot wind coming off the highway reminded me that summer was coming to an end, and a new season was about to be born.

7

After school, I met James to haul off a tree we cut down over the summer. We made a little extra cash taking on odd jobs, mostly trucking stuff to the dump for old ladies. When I showed up he was dragging a limb toward a trailer. With me on crutches I could only help so much, but the job had been scheduled before the injury.

"Hey," he said. "What's wrong with you?"

I got out of the truck and found my work gloves in the toolbox. "What?"

"Your phone is still off. You giving me the cold shoulder because of this Villarreal stuff?"

"You left me lying there in the road."

"Hell yeah. And you saved us, pal. Everybody knows it. Everybody. No one is ever going to forget that for as long as we live. This is good for you."

He heaved the end of the trunk onto the lip of the trailer. I crutched over to help him.

"We ought to contract some freshmen to do this," he said. "Then not pay them."

We double-teamed the trunk into the corner of the trailer.

"I'll be honest, man. I don't feel like it's good for me. I feel like I have some flakey friends and a broken ankle. And that I'm missing the football season because of you. That's what I feel like."

He paused and took off his cap, offended. In that moment, something between us changed forever. We both noticed at the same time and both pretended not to. He grinned and slapped my shoulder.

"I don't know. That seems like the wrong attitude. Think of all the time you'll have now to hang out with us. We miss seeing you, man. These girls this year . . . I'm telling you, it's like a fever. You say 'senior year' and like magic they do anything. I mean, anything."

I knew what he meant, but lately my romantic thoughts were for Noa alone. I highly-doubted that she had the same strand of senior fever as James did.

"I don't know how much I'll be able to help you move this stuff," I said. "But I wanted to follow through."

"That's okay. We got the heavy one. I can get the rest."

He took a fold of cash out of his front pocket and gave me a hundred bucks.

"Half is too much."

"Don't worry about it. We're partners. You take one for me, I take one for you. That's how it works."

"Thanks."

I headed back to my truck and fired it up. Just before driving off, James tapped on the passenger window. I rolled it down.

"You're friends with that girl Noa, right?"

"Yeah. Why?"

"Miles is taking her on a date. Isn't that hilarious? He thinks she's hot now. I warned him she's a band dork."

"Wait. What'd you say?"

"Miles and Noa. They're going out."

"Where are they going?"

"I don't know. He said his parents are gone for the week-end, so maybe they won't be going anywhere." James grinned. "Anyways, I'll call you. I want you in the loop. Keep your phone on."

I felt sick.

8

By chance I ran into Wayne at the grocery store.

His cart was filled with lunchmeat and white bread. He said his family required ten pounds of thick-sliced ham every week. I asked how that could be possible and he said on Mondays, Wednesdays, and Saturdays they ate sandwiches for lunch and supper. When I told him about Noa and Miles, he came up with the idea of stalking them on their date. I wished he didn't use the word 'stalk' because it made us sound like the bad guys, but I agreed to the idea. All we had to do was stop by his house for binoculars and an electric stun gun in case Miles charged us. I told him I could handle Miles one on one, but Wayne wished for a little extra protection since I was hobbled.

Miles was a rotten apple. Junior year a girl said he groped her in the football training room, but it came down to his word versus hers. He skated free. The last thing I wanted was for Noa to be in the same situation.

I could protect her.

Wayne's dad, Burt, helped us locate the stun gun in his nightstand and told us to have a good time and be home by morning. He showed us how to work it with the right voltage based on a man's weight.

Then he said, "Ah screw it. Just don't hit anyone in the heart. I'd hate for you boys to wind up in prison over something like this."

He cranked the power up all the way and tossed it to Wayne.

The walls of the double-wide were decorated with photos of Burt's prized muscle cars over the years and a framed report card from one of Wayne's little brothers who earned straight As.

"Who's gettin' shocked?" he asked, cracking open a Budweiser.

"Some guy stole Colt's girlfriend so we're going after him."

"Oh," he said. "In that case I'd aim for the nuts. Let him feel the sting on his ding-a-ling."

We took Wayne's car and listened to Mexican music with the windows down. He stuffed a pipe full of tobacco and lit the top with a match.

"That Lucas guy is wild," he said. "I'm going back this week."

"Me too."

"Thanks for inviting me to come. I didn't know what to expect."

"Me either."

"He got me thinking about life and what we're doing and all that. I wrote some stuff down in the journal he gave me."

"I haven't yet but I'm going to," I said.

"It was weird," Wayne mused aloud. "Sunday night after the graveyard, I dreamed about a long road going into the desert and me driving a hundred miles an hour thinking I had all this road left to go. And before I knew it the car and me just went right off a cliff into the rocks. Poof. I'm dead. That's what I wrote about. You want some of this?"

He passed me the pipe.

"It's called 'Midnight Rain.' They have all kinds of names at the tobacco shop. Me and Lucas went together."

"Oh. Have y'all been hanging out?"

"We just smoked pipes and went back to the cemetery to walk around and talk."

We parked across the street from the ice cream parlor. Sure enough, Noa and Miles sat on the hood of his Jeep eating ice cream. I felt a punch in my gut watching them. Even worse, it seemed like she was having a pretty good time.

Wayne looked through the binoculars. With the stun gun on the dash, he resembled a rookie cop thanks to his rough, wild sideburns.

"You like this jerk-off Miles?"

"No."

"Me either," he said. "So you and Noa, huh? I didn't see that one coming."

"We aren't boyfriend and girlfriend or anything."

"You like her though? She's pretty, man. Real pretty. Always has been. And nice too. Screw this late-bloomer talk. I've seen it since day one, which is one of my rare gifts. We had science class together last year and she volunteered to be my lab partner even though it was a group grade. *Nobody* wanted to be my partner. Nobody. Because of me she got a C."

"Yeah. I like her."

That's the first time I told anyone out loud. Noa must have known she had my heart on a string. Then again maybe she felt confused because I never said what I needed to say. I realized how I felt wouldn't matter much if I never spoke the words. I could love her like Romeo loved Juliet, but at some point you have to stand up and say so or else you just cruise off the cliff like Wayne did in his dream. Or, one day you're sitting in a parking lot watching her fall in love with someone else.

"Here. See for yourself."

Wayne handed me the binoculars in time for me to see Miles try and place his hand on Noa's thigh. She brushed his hand away.

"What do we do?" Wayne asked. "Should we stun him? Really give him a scare?"

"I don't know."

"Come on, man, *think*!"

Wayne sped things along by holding down the car horn for ten straight seconds.

We both sank into the seats so they couldn't see. After a minute passed with us laughing, we peeked through the windshield. Wayne honked again. This time when we looked up, Noa was crossing the street toward us. She let a car pass then ran to us in her wedge shoes.

She knocked on the window. Wayne rolled it down, both of us still crouched in the seats.

"Hi, Noa."

"Hi, Noa."

"Hi. I'm wondering what on earth you're doing here."

"Just out for a drive," I said. "Wayne's horn stopped working so we wanted to test it out."

Wayne held a hand over his face.

"It seems to be working now," I added.

"Well, you geniuses parked under a streetlight, so I can see right through the windshield. And I don't appreciate you watching me with binoculars like a couple of perverts."

Wayne covered the stun gun with a shop towel.

"We were out for a drive and saw you and just stopped to

see what was going on."

Noa brushed the hair from her face and waved at Miles to let him know she was okay.

"How about this? Wayne, Colt, I'm a big girl and can take care of myself. So if you don't want someone taking me out on a date then one of you should have asked me. Until then, don't blame anybody but yourselves."

She made a point to shoot her eyes at me, then marched back across the street. I had to give her credit. She wasn't shy about giving me a hint. Miles opened the car door for her then flipped us off with both hands raised high. They sped through an intersection then whipped onto Valley Mills Drive.

"Should we tail them?" Wayne asked.

"No. I hate to say it, but I think she's right."

The night wasn't a total waste. We went to an empty parking lot and practiced shooting the stun gun at each other with the voltage on the lowest level. I hit Wayne in the throat and laughed so hard I nearly choked to death.

9

At the circle the next Sunday night, Lucas opened up with a prayer. He sounded like a wise old Cherokee medicine man, talking about the beauty of the moon feeding our souls and other mysterious ideas.

Then he asked us to take out our journals and share our conclusions from last week's question: *Why are you here?*

Peter Dietrich went first. He wrote one clean sentence.

"We are here on earth to follow God until we are called home to heaven."

"Okay," Lucas said. "But why are you here tonight? Sitting with us? You could be anywhere, and your choices have led you here."

Peter closed his journal.

"My family has always come to church. Like, forever."

"Is that your decision or a decision that is made for you?"

"I guess I just get in the car. And we come here."

"What would happen if you chose to stay home?"

Peter pulled his collar.

"I don't think my mom would like that very much."

"What if you told her it wasn't her decision to make?"

"I think she'd make me anyway."

"When you move out of her house—assuming that you do—are you going to call her every time you do or don't go to church?"

"I guess not."

"It's time to become your own man, Peter. To claim your life, thoughts, and heart as your own. But nothing will be revealed to you until you start seeking."

Peter scanned the circle for a translator. He sported a crew cut of feather brown hair and tucked his shirt into his sailboat-patterned shorts. He was the kind of guy who showed up ten minutes early and ate everything on his plate, even raw vegetables. His dad died fighting in Afghanistan, and if you looked closely, you could see the outline of a dog tag on a silver chain beneath his shirt.

Lucas warmed his hands over the fire.

"Hey, Lucas, what do you believe about God?" Wayne asked.

Everybody wanted to know. From day one, we couldn't tell if he was an atheist or the most devout Christian we had ever met. He wouldn't let us see one way or the other.

"Does it matter?"

"It does to me," Peter said.

"Me too," said Malik.

Lucas gazed up at the stars, then back to Wayne.

"'God' is a word that means many different things to many different people. Tell me what the word means to you, and I can tell you if I believe in that interpretation of the word 'God.'"

Wayne fumbled through an explanation, but finally gave up and said, "I'm not good at explaining religious stuff."

"Neither am I," Lucas said. He returned to his original question. "Why are you guys here?"

Everyone went around and read passages from their journals. Wayne believed with certainty that his dream about flying off the cliff at a hundred miles per hour would come to pass, so he said he had a lot of living to do before dying. Then he got into how he'd like to dance with a pretty girl on a secluded beach in Mexico.

Everyone came to varying conclusions. Mostly, parents made them come to church.

"Colt, you've been quiet," Lucas said. "Did you write anything?"

"No. I forgot."

"Why did you get into your car and drive here tonight? Why are you spending your precious hours of life sitting with us under the stars? Why aren't you somewhere else?"

I flipped a few blank pages of my journal as if maybe I answered the question and forgot.

"I guess I want to be around something true," I said.

"And what makes something true?"

The guys waited, probably grateful Lucas saved these questions for me and not them.

"It's just that—I honestly don't really know what to do with my life right now," I said. "I don't know why I'm here just like I don't know why I'm anywhere. It's like I'm sleepwalking through everything. I want to wake up."

"I understand," he said. "But that doesn't tell me why you're here."

In that moment, I wished Lucas had never interrupted my life. And made me say this out loud.

"Because I want to *live*, man. I want my life to mean something. I don't know what you want me to say."

Lucas nodded, then took a long drag on his pipe.

"That's the most important decision you'll ever make. To *live*."

10

One thing no one warned me about senior year is that everybody's mother wants to throw their kid a party.

So every week it seemed I got a new invitation in the mail to send off so and so to the school they picked for college. Usually, it was a backyard barbecue or a bowling party, but a handful were memorable, rambunctious affairs, with none more so than the Foam Party at the Community Center. I'd never been to a foam party, but from what I heard the basketball gym would be filled floor to ceiling with slick bubbles and we'd be disoriented by strobe lights and rap music. Everybody was pretty excited about it.

I tried to take Noa as my date but she had a jazz club performance and would be coming late.

James and his crew stopped by my house before the party to pick me up, but I told them I planned to ride with Wayne.

"Wayne Derrick?"

"Yeah."

"You're serious right now?" James asked. "Wayne Derrick?"

"I already told him we could ride together."

James looked back at his truck packed with people.

"Does Wayne have beautiful girlies in his car? Does Wayne have a margarita machine plugged into his AC outlet?"

"We'll catch up when I get there."

"What's up with you lately?"

"Nothing. Just meeting new people. Senior year."

"Yeah. You're right. You should stay the night at my house. Pack a bag."

Wayne arrived a half hour later with a cooler full of pre-made tacos the Mexican joint by his house gave to his family instead of throwing them in the garbage. We sat on my back porch dumping salsa on the rubbery beef to hide the flavor. Amado and Malik and Charlie showed up too, and there we sat, hanging out for the first time as friends. Wayne passed out the tacos and lit up his pipe.

"Where did Lucas even come from?" he asked. "This guy is out of this world."

None of us knew. I told them about the book, and how I thought it was some kind of sign.

"Y'all can't say anything," Malik said, leaning forward. "But I heard something about him."

He let the tension build and took a bite of a taco.

"He killed a guy."

"Shut up. That's not true."

"I swear that's what I heard."

Wayne burst into laughter.

"You don't seriously believe that."

Malik shrugged.

"All I know is that it was someone at his school."

"If he killed someone, he'd be in prison," Wayne challenged.

"Unless he got off somehow. I'm just saying he could be

anyone. Nobody knows who he is or where he came from."

We put the investigation on hold to solve another day and piled into Malik's car to go to the foam party.

Apparently we missed the memo that it was a costume party, but only about half of the people were dressed up. Walking through the front doors I passed by Batman and Miss America making out. Inside, I pushed through a thick wall of foam. Music blasted from the nothingness. I wandered around able to see about six inches in front of my face and by luck bumped into Noa after an hour or so.

"I've been looking for you," she said. She wore a headband with black pointed ears.

"What's up with the ears?" I asked.

"I'm a cat."

"I didn't know this was a costume party."

"Then you didn't read the invitation."

"That's your cat costume?"

She straightened the ears on her head, now feeling self-conscious.

"Oh, and you must be a washed-up football player with a busted ankle."

I grinned.

"You got me."

A dancing couple rammed into us from the mass of foam. I caught Noa to keep her from falling. She burst into laughter at the craziness of it all. We could hardly see anything or anyone, but I knew we were surrounded on all sides. I had to shout over the music for her to hear me, which also caused us to be close. She danced a little to the music, and I couldn't tell if she wanted me to dance with her or not.

I drummed up some courage.

"So, I've been meaning to ask you something. I don't know if you have plans or what, but would you ever want to go out on a real date? Maybe next weekend? I think it could be fun to hang out just the two of us. Someplace we can actually hear each other."

She nodded. "Yeah, I think I'm free. What do you want to do?"

Without thinking, I said, "It's a surprise. Dress up nice."

She moved closer to me and clasped her hands behind my neck.

Just then, Wayne leapt through the foam. He grabbed my collar.

"Get out here. Now!"

"What?"

"Charlie is about to get his nuts stuffed up his butt."

I trailed him through the foam with Noa holding my hand.

We went out the front doors and into the parking lot where a crowd had gathered. Charlie and James circled each other. James pawed at a split lip. His shirt was streaked with blood.

"Get in there and say something," Wayne said.

I hobbled between them and stepped in front of James, holding him back.

"Easy…"

"Back up," James said. "This guy is dead. He's dead."

Charlie was thin as a rail but angry as a bull. James outweighed him by at least fifty pounds.

"What's going on?"

Neither would say. Then I saw Charlie's little sister in the crowd and put the pieces of the puzzle together. If I had looked closely at James's car earlier, I would have seen her in the back seat sipping a margarita.

Turned out that Charlie had bumped into the two of them dancing. James's hands were wandering all over her. Before James knew what was going on, Charlie walloped him in the face and bit his arm like a feral dog. They scuffled through the crowded foam and out to the parking lot.

"Slow down, Charlie," I said.

"I'm going to kill him."

"Easy, pal. You want the cops to come?"

"Yeah," he said. "I want them to arrest this bastard. I want them to clean his blood off my hands and from my teeth."

He'd lost his mind. He hollered at James, and no one understood what he said.

James glanced back at Charlie's sister. "Honestly, bro, she's a prude anyways. And flat as a board."

Charlie charged but I caught his arm and told him to back down.

Then I turned to James.

"Call it off. I'm serious. You mess with him and you mess with me. Let it go."

The crowd booed.

"Knock his ass out, James!" Miles called.

"Everyone shut up!" I said. "This is over. Go back inside."

James breathed on my right cheek with Charlie breathing on my left. They glared right through me at each other.

"Fine," James said. "I don't need to prove anything. He knows where to find me."

He blew a kiss at Charlie to provoke him. James got into his truck and slammed the door shut. He rolled down the window as I walked toward him.

"I didn't realize you were so soft," he said.

"I'm trying to save you from being an idiot."

"Yeah? Is that your job now? To save me? How about you and your new boyfriends go get in your circle and write a poem about it."

He hawked a loogie at Charlie and sped away. Well, that sent Charlie over the edge. He chased after the truck, but Wayne caught hold of his shirttail. When that didn't work, Wayne unholstered the stun gun and gave Charlie a charge, sending him to the pavement. Wayne dragged Charlie off into the distance and bear-hugged him to the ground. He held him there for ten or twelve minutes until Charlie's breathing regulated.

Most people went back to the chaos of the foam. Our crew decided to call it a night. Noa the cat drove us home. I rolled down the window and felt the air in my face and the fire in my soul.

If life was changing, I was ready.

11

At the circle on Sunday night, everybody had a story to tell from the foam party, most of them X-rated and all of them half-true. The only thing we all remembered with certainty was the fight between James and Charlie.

Charlie had bought a pipe just like Wayne's, and they both dug into a sack of tobacco that sat on Wayne's tailgate. Charlie lit it up and coughed then walked off to be alone with his thoughts. He told someone that he was going to murder James if given the opportunity. I chalked it up to high passions that would fade over time. Or maybe he would do it. I didn't know him all that well, and he certainly went crazy in the parking lot until Wayne zapped him.

Lucas hadn't shown up yet, so we talked openly about the unlikely couples we saw kissing and grinding against each other in the foam. We all knew a general idea of each other's romantic histories, with a few exceptions. Amado and Malik were the kinds of guys who suggested truth or dare at mixed gatherings, Wayne spent a lot of high-profile effort overcompensating for the blue wiener rumor, Charlie had a girlfriend for our whole junior year but dumped her when she started talking about getting married, and Ortiz hung around with a few middle-aged ladies he met while fixing their websites.

Peter stayed quiet in the back of his mom's minivan.

"Peter, who was the first girl you ever kissed?" Wayne asked.

Peter's face got red.

"Oh," Ortiz said.

"I thought y'all had homeschool rallies and stuff like that," Wayne kept on. "Plus I had a third cousin who was homeschooled and she got pregnant when she was fifteen. From another homeschool kid. Apparently they didn't even know what was happening. I figured you would have kissed a girl by now with your looks."

I nudged Wayne's ribs for him to lay off.

"I'm serious. Homeschool kids are *freaky-deaky*."

"It's okay," Peter said. "I never really had a chance."

"You ever liked somebody?"

"I guess. I don't know."

"You ever spent time on a dirty website? I can point you in the right direction."

"No thank you," Peter said. "I had a girlfriend and we did lots of . . . *other stuff*. But she didn't want to kiss."

We tried to put together the sequence of events, which usually started with the kissing then progressed to 'other stuff.' We all sat for a minute in bewilderment.

"What do you mean other stuff?" Malik asked.

He held all of our attention. Charlie moseyed back to the circle to hear the answer.

"Just . . . *stuff*."

Lucas drove up, his headlights interrupting the confessional.

"Did everyone wear tennis shoes like I said?" he asked.

We all did.

"Get a light. Follow me."

In his front seat we found a mixed collection of flashlights and each of us claimed one. Lucas ran off toward the highway with his beam of light bouncing. We followed breathless, with me hopping along at the tail end of the group.

About a quarter mile away we came to a two-lane bridge that crossed over a freeway. Lucas clicked off the light. He waited until no cars were coming then ducked underneath the bridge and shuffled into the darkness. We inched down the slope of concrete and heard Lucas whisper for us to come underneath the bridge. Cars whizzed past on the freeway below. I made it okay despite the boot on my foot, and Wayne made sure I didn't topple to my death. We all huddled together in a concrete rafter.

"Don't make too much noise," Lucas said. "The cops come down here every once in a while."

"Is it illegal? Are we trespassing?" Peter asked.

He shined his light down the length of the bridge.

"Turn it off!"

Peter clicked it off.

"Keep your voices down. This is a sanctuary."

Of course, no one knew what Lucas meant. A car drove on the bridge and the concrete rumbled over our heads.

"If a cop ever comes down here, tell him you heard a weird noise and just came to check it out. Play dumb. We can't jeopardize this place."

Lucas clicked on his flashlight and pressed it into the concrete so only a sliver of light came through.

"I used to come down here when I was your age. Seems like yesterday in some ways, and lifetimes ago in others."

He opened the light enough to reveal faded writing on the walls, along with his name and a date from seven years prior. He held up the light to show how the words he had written in black marker had faded over time. I could barely make out an Emerson quote that said, "What lies behind you and what lies in front of you, pales in comparison to what lies within you." The quotes looked like a chalkboard in a crazed mathematician's private lair.

"I covered the walls of this rafter with words that inspired me. I let them fill up my soul. A lot of times, I came here in the middle of the night and watched the cars pass by on the highway, wondering where they had been and where they were going. Each person has a different story to tell. A different struggle. A different journey they are taking. Look."

Lucas clicked off the flashlight and we stood in the silence.

A single car came up the freeway and disappeared into the distance.

"This is your mission: Come back this week by yourself and fill these walls with quotes that inspire your own hearts. It can be a line from a book, movie, scripture, anything. Whatever it is, make sure the words you write can last forever. Because even though they may fade from these walls, as the words I wrote when I was your age have faded, they still live in my heart. I carry them in every breath."

Lucas took out a black marker and wrote today's date at the top of the rafter. Then each of us signed our names beside his.

"This is your sanctuary now," he said. "Make of it what you will."

He eased through the group of guys and walked up the side of the bridge.

We tried to follow him back to the church but he was gone, moving like a mist through the nearby woods.

*

Later that night I couldn't sleep.

So I snuck out of the house and made the long walk back to the bridge.

I pulled a black marker from my pocket and found a clear spot on the concrete. That's where I wrote the Emerson quote in block letters: "If the stars should appear one night in a thousand years, how would men believe and adore; and preserve for many generations the remembrance of the city of God which had been shown! But every night come out these envoys of beauty, and light the universe with their admonishing smile."

Then I watched cars go down the highway. I wondered where they came from and where they were going. I wondered what stories they carried with them.

I wondered how much time they had left.

12

One way I could cut a few days off my ISS sentence was to volunteer in the reading lab at the junior high. Villareal forgot to share that little detail with me, but a few of my mom's PTA friends let her in on the secret. So for the last week I had been paired up with a bucktooth seventh grader named Harold.

I made the mistake of telling him I had a date.

"Take her to the snow cone stand," Harold suggested. "Chicks love shaved ice."

"She already went out for ice cream on her last date, Harold."

"Snow cones are different than ice cream."

"Not different enough. Plus, if it's a date, I can't take her to a snow cone stand. That's junior high stuff."

I sat with Harold in the reading lab going through his reading homework.

"How am I supposed to know?" he asked. "I've never even been on a date."

"Exactly. That's my point."

I read over the sheet his teacher sent, with the assigned page numbers highlighted in yellow.

"We need to get through ten pages before you leave."

He took out his book called *The Outsiders* and I sort of remembered it from when I was in the seventh grade.

Harold's hurdle was the big reading comprehension test. He'd failed as many times as he had taken it. Apparently they took all their tests in the computer lab and earned points for each book they read. If you got enough points, they gave you a pair of striped socks and a colored pen, stuff like that. Harold told me the kid who read the most books by the end of the year would drive a fire truck around the parking lot with everyone watching, a prize he desperately wanted. At this rate, I had a better shot at being named the next Pope.

Harold paused every once in a while and pointed at words he couldn't understand. I'd say the word aloud, tell him what it meant, and have him copy down the word in his notepad.

"This Ponyboy is going to get himself in deep trouble," Harold said.

"That's what makes a good story. The characters get themselves in trouble and have to find their way out of it."

"It's because of his older brothers."

"You got any brothers and sisters?"

"I have an older brother," Harold said. "But he's sort of an asshole."

"Hey."

The teacher glanced over. I waved in apology.

"You're going to get us both kicked out of here."

"He stays in his room a lot and always says he's going to kill everybody. They put him on some pills, but he doesn't take them."

"What's his name?"

"Presley."

"Presley Thomas?" I asked.

"Yeah. You know him?"

"He's in my grade."

"Well, I'd stay *really* far away from him."

Presley was a quiet kid who mostly kept to himself. I sat next to him on a field trip a long time ago and we talked about a television show where a lady won a million dollars. I got the feeling that our conversation was important to him, somehow. Since then we always said hello in the halls but nothing more. He wore baggy black jeans and t-shirts featuring obscure heavy metal bands.

"So where you going to take her? This Noa girl."

"I don't know. Maybe a movie?"

"You can't talk in movies. You going to kiss her?"

"That's none of your business."

"So, negative."

"Maybe."

"Then just go down to the park and roll up the windows. That's what I'd do. Put on some rap and start kissing like . . ."

He imitated a couple kissing, wrapping his hands around his own shoulders and wagging his tongue.

"Okay. Shut up and read."

I took out my Emerson book. Most of the passages went over my head but I marked a few to re-read. Some of the lines deserved a place on the bridge.

The past weeks of the sacred circle had been the strangest and most wonderful nights of my life. We talked about dying, and Peter admitted he was more afraid of dying than anything else, even though he believed in going to heaven. Lucas challenged him, "If you believe in an afterlife, then why are you afraid to die? If you really think your soul will continue on after this existence, then why do you live with any fear?" That threw Peter for a loop.

He was quiet for a while, then spoke up again and said he believed in heaven with all his heart but didn't want to die because he dreaded putting his mom through losing another loved one after his dad died. At that point we all broke down and hugged on Peter.

"Hey, Colt?" Harold asked.

"Yeah?"

"How come you're doing this? Helping me learn to read good and all that."

I thought about it. "I don't really know. I guess I'm trying to do something that matters, for once."

"Well . . . thanks," Harold said, then took a deep, pensive breath. "I'm only here because I have to be."

"Yeah. I know."

After tutoring ended, I crossed the parking lot toward my car. A few rows away, I saw James sitting in his car, the windows halfway down. I couldn't tell for sure, but it seemed like he was watching me in the rearview mirror. Maybe I should have gone over to make amends.

But I didn't.

13

"I feel like I'm overdressed," Noa said as soon as she saw me standing in the doorway. She wore a silky navy dress and heels. I wore blue jeans, a t-shirt, and a ball cap.

"I can't say one way or the other."

"Colt. Seriously. Should I change?"

"No. Please. You look so pretty I don't want you to."

"What are we doing?"

"You'll see. It's not a big deal. I promise."

"Well you could have told me that."

So, not a great start to the date.

She sighed as we walked to my truck parked on the street. I opened the door for her and ran around to the other side.

"You can start off by picking the music," I said.

"Are we picking music for going out to a nice restaurant, or to a theme park, or a wedding, or a concert? Because I don't know where we're going and it's sort of making me crazy."

"Pick something that makes you happy."

She found a jazz station.

Noa pulled down the visor and checked her makeup in the small mirror. She applied some lip gloss. Ever since I figured out what I wanted to do, I kept our date a mystery. I meant to call and update her on what to wear. Honestly, I forgot. And now, she looked so good I didn't want her to change. But I saw her point. She was going to feel ridiculous.

"You missed the football game last night," she said.

"Who won?"

"The other team. You don't think you should be there for the guys?"

"Wayne had a few of us over to burn a pile of trash in his backyard. I was planning on going but by the time we got done and I remembered, it was after ten o'clock."

She lifted her eyebrows and went back to putting on makeup in the mirror.

"Just so you know, I didn't eat anything. So if we aren't going to a restaurant, do you mind if we stop and grab something?"

"Hang on. What was that look for?"

"Nothing," she said.

"Tell me."

"People noticed you weren't there."

"So what?"

"It's just that I heard what some people were saying about you."

"Who?"

"I don't want to get in the middle of anything but people noticed you weren't there and they sort of made a big deal about it."

"James?"

"Really, don't say anything. They're so stupid."

I pulled into a fast-food joint.

"Feel free to order whatever you want. As long as it's under five bucks." She turned to make sure I was kidding around. "I promise I have something special planned. But you eat three times a day, so I figured we could do something that's a little more unique. We need to get where we're going."

After we picked up the food, I rolled down the windows and took her out to my grandparents' house. They lived outside of town on twenty acres. They had been traveling the southwest via RV for a few months so I knew they wouldn't be there. They kept a key to the barn under a flowerpot on the porch and I knew that they still owned a go-kart that was primed and ready to go. Me and my brothers used to ride that thing from sunup to sundown, and it was amazing the engine hadn't blown. I walked her across the barn to an army green canvas that was covering the go-kart.

"Are you ready?"

"Should I be nervous right now?" she asked.

Of all the places she expected to go, I bet a barn in the middle of the country was low on her list. The corners of the barn were layered with spiderwebs and we were surrounded by rusty tools, slowly coming into focus as the lights above us came to full strength.

"Underneath this is a magical machine so spectacular that you will never be the same. Tonight, your life will change forever."

"Okay. I think I'm ready."

"Beneath this . . ."

She whipped it off and saw the go-kart.

A moment passed where I wondered if I'd made a huge mistake. She held the dusty canvas in one hand, and I'll never forget the way the silky dress looked next to it.

"Noa . . ."

A smile crept across her face.

"Oh . . . It is so on. Let's ride!"

"Yes!"

We found a couple of spotlights in the barn and duct-taped them to the roll cage. I cranked the engine and it sputtered for a moment before roaring to life.

"Wait. Do we need helmets?" she asked.

"Right . . ." I rifled through a bin and pulled out two helmets.

I brushed off the spider webs and tossed one to her. She pulled the helmet over her hair and sat in the passenger's seat, her dress balled up in her hand. I clicked on the spotlights. They beamed into the darkness beyond the open barn door. I sat down beside her, having to yell over the growl of the engine.

"There's no turning back," I hollered. "And there's no guarantee we'll make it out of this alive."

She glanced over at me. I could see the smile of her eyes through the slit of the helmet.

"You only live once!"

She flipped the visor down and stared ahead.

I hit the pedal and we shot into the darkness like a rocket, rumbling over the uneven ground and bouncing through the trees. She screamed in terror and then said to go faster, faster, and maybe that's when I fell in love. We burned around that old homemade racetrack now overgrown with tall grass, but I knew the turns well enough to stay upright. I probably could have driven that track with my eyes closed.

On our second lap, we hit a rough patch and the two spotlights tumbled in our wake. I rolled the cart to a stop. Sitting there in the pitch black, I flipped the ignition off.

We took off our helmets, both of us sweaty and breathing heavy.

My heart pounded and I knew that the time had come.

I leaned over and kissed her.

14

We showed up at the church with our bags packed for a camping trip. The plan was to watch a movie on the big screen in the youth room and then load up in the trucks and hit the road for our campout.

For the past few weeks, the group had been growing. We started out with just me, Ortiz, Charlie, Wayne, Peter, Malik, and Amado. But now Nate and Santino were in the mix too. Nate took photographs for the school newspaper and won a couple of high-profile contests in major magazines. He had a website and everything. I heard a rumor that he made a thousand dollars a month selling posters of his photographs. Since joining the group, he had already photographed the bridge and taken black-and-white portraits of our faces for a new series he titled *Elements*. We made him swear not to show anybody. Santino came from a super-rich family. He suffered from a lifelong stutter. But his family owned a few thousand acres outside of town, so we figured we could go camping on his land.

We all settled into the youth room and Lucas fooled around with the sound and video boards in the back. Ortiz walked in with two ten-gallon sacks of popcorn and a duffel bag of soda cans. He cracked open a root beer and put his feet up on a chair. Wayne lit his pipe. Lucas glanced up.

"All right, guys. Take it easy for a while. No smoking pipes in the church. I had to go out of my way to get Gideon to let us do this."

Everyone snuffed out their pipes as the lights faded and the movie started.

The movie was called *Dead Poets Society*, about some prep school kids who started a poetry club. One of them committed suicide when his dad wouldn't let him be an actor in the school play. Even though the story was depressing, it was actually really good. I know for a fact Wayne cried because he sat next to me sniffling and blowing his nose into his shirtsleeve. The movie hit Santino like a ton of bricks since his own dad put pressure on him to be a winner but always called him a 'born loser'.

Lucas turned on the lights after the credits finished.

He sat down on the stage and faced us as we went around saying which character we most related to in the movie. It was interesting to hear who picked who.

Lucas sat facing us, heavy in thought.

"One day, you'll have a dream," he said. "It will start as a small campfire in your heart, and over time that fire will grow .. . and grow . . . and grow until it consumes your thoughts. When you go to sleep, you will dream of that fire. When you wake, you will do whatever you can to feed the flame. Your life will take shape around the dream. The choices you make. The people who come in and out of your orbit. The fire determines everything. Maybe you'll want to climb Mount Everest, or find a cure for cancer, or build a cabin in the woods with your bare hands. Each of you will be called into your own journey — a sacred calling—and you must choose whether or not you will accept the invitation. And the only way to know with certainty the dream is worth chasing is that others in your life will tell you it's too risky. Too irresponsible. They'll guide you to a safer path and say, 'Look, this is easier.' They'll busy you with meaningless tasks and obligations. They'll encourage you to pursue the dream in your free time, or when you get older. They'll point at others who have set sail on stormy seas and never come home. But as we know, time waits on no one. Tomorrow, we're already dead."

Malik ripped a fart.

We burst into laughter, even Lucas.

"All right, clean this place up. Let's go set up camp."

We picked up the stray popcorn and went down the stairwell to the parking lot.

Amado was the first one out and caused a pileup in the doorway when he came to a dead stop.

Every single one of our cars dripped with eggs, and the windows were shoe-polished with dirty words. Not to mention our tires were flat to the ground.

"What the hell, man," Wayne said, rushing to his car. He left the windows down so the eggs splattered all over his CD collection. "My music!"

The guys sprinted to their cars to check the damage. Peter took off his shirt and used it to wipe the big white boners off his mom's minivan. Ortiz calmly took an emergency roadside kit out of his car to inflate our tires. Nate drove an open-air Jeep and the eggs crept into the cracks of his camera case. They wrote 'DICKWAD' on my front windshield with a circle over the driver and 'QUITTER' on the back, to go along with a couple dozen eggs smashed into the air vent.

"You have any idea who would do this?" Lucas asked.

"Yeah," I said. "I think I do."

15

After first period I met Wayne at his locker. He slammed it shut.

"What's wrong with you?" I asked.

"This."

He handed me a folded-up report card full of failing grades.

"When we get out of here they'll let us use something called calculators. Who gives a damn if I can't do long division? They want us to do all this bullcrap without asking some basic questions, like how on earth is knowing about particles in outer space going to help me make a living one day. And to top it off we get locked in here with a bunch of jerk-offs."

"Easy . . ."

"Here's what I think about long division."

He took out his pipe matches and set the report card on fire, then let it fall to the tile floor. Wayne leaned in close.

"We have the whole world right at our fingers, pal. I mean right here. And guys like me and you can go anywhere and do anything. We can chase dreams, just like Lucas says. We can travel around the whole world and pick up odd jobs along the way. So what are we wasting our time in this place for, Colt?

Give me one good reason we aren't sailing a ship across the Atlantic Ocean or dancing with pretty girls in Mexico?"

There he went again with the pretty girls in Mexico.

"You can't drop out."

"Why not?"

"'Cause then I'd still be here and wouldn't have anyone to talk to."

He nodded.

"At least give it another six weeks and see if things get better."

I offered my hand and he reluctantly shook it.

We turned to go to class. James and his crew were walking in front of us. I could tell they were talking about throwing eggs at our cars because of how they laughed. James made a throwing motion and then showed how the egg splattered against the glass. Villarreal stood on the second floor, hovering over the halls like a gargoyle. Wayne sped up.

"Where you going?"

"Watch and see."

I tried to catch his shirt but it was pointless.

Wayne speared James to the ground and wailed on him like Mike Tyson. I mean he really beat him up. Wayne pinned him down and between blows shouted, "Why. Are. You. Such. A. Jackass!" By the time some of the other guys threw him off, James was bloodied and missing a tooth.

This started the brawl of the century.

Charlie came running out of nowhere and instead of helping Wayne, who had his hands full with a couple guys, he doubled down on James and made good on his promise to strangle him. Charlie's sister saw the whole thing. She screamed at the top of her lungs. That's when Tyler Cooper punched me in the back of the head. Just like that I was in the middle of it all too. I don't remember how many guys I punched or how many guys punched me. At one point me and Amado had each other in a headlock and then realized it and went for different people. Even Nate and Santino joined in at the last minute. I didn't see this part with my own eyes, but everyone said Santino kicked a few guys like Jackie Chan. Turned out, he was a black belt in Tae Kwon Do. The fight seemed to last an hour but in retrospect only a minute passed before Villarreal bullied his way into the center of the chaos and put Wayne into a submission hold. Wayne twisted and bucked like a champion bull but eventually blacked out.

Villarreal stood up breathing heavy. He looked down on Wayne's limp body.

"Don't worry about him," he said, sounding pretty worried. "He's unconscious, but still alive."

Everybody in school had gathered by this point. The tardy bell rang. No one moved. No one said a word. James took the worst of it. Blood came out of his mouth and made a big triangle down to his waist.

"Get to class!" Villarreal announced in a faltering voice to the crowd. "Get out of here before I put you all in detention!"

Wayne came to and rubbed his eyes.

Villarreal figured out the two sides of the fight pretty easily and mostly dismissed the bystanders. He put our group in one classroom and James's group in another. We stayed there all day, unable to speak or work on homework. They allowed us to stare at the chalkboard, under the supervision of Coach Julip. Every half hour or so they called someone new to the office to face interrogation.

Villarreal called everyone else before me, and finally showed up in the doorway at four p.m.

"Hey, Colt, let's go."

I gathered my stuff and followed him down the empty halls. He led me to the front entrance.

"I was really counting on you to be a leader this year," he said, pushing open the front door. "Boy was I wrong."

16

I had an invitation to another senior party that night but I decided to stay home. This one was being held at a mini golf course and I didn't feel like having my head whacked with a putter. I escaped the brawl with no real injuries minus a sore jaw.

At the dinner table my mom stared at me until I said, "Yes?"

"Don't you have something you want to tell us?"

I looked over at my dad, who gave no indication what she was talking about.

"Not that I know of."

"Colt. Seriously?"

"I don't know what you mean, Mom."

She hit me with her napkin.

"You and Noa! She's precious. I can't believe you took her on a date and didn't even tell us. Is she your girlfriend? Officially, I mean."

"Oh. I don't know."

"What do you mean you don't know?"

"I don't know."

"Well, have you asked her to be your girlfriend?"

"Nobody asks someone if they want to be their girlfriend,"

I said. "It just sort of happens."

She motioned at my dad to step in and offer some much-needed wisdom.

"You like this girl, right?" he asked.

"Yes."

"And she likes you back?"

"I think so," I answered.

My mom butted back in. "Yes! At least that's what her mom said."

"Why are you talking to her mom?"

"I happened to run into her at a PTA thing and we got to talking. Not just about y'all. About a lot of things." She turned to my dad. "She likes him."

"Okay, easy as that. You ask her to be your girlfriend."

My little brother died laughing.

"Just don't miss your chance, Colt. She's a doll." She paused. "Is your jaw swollen?"

I shook my head. "I don't think so. Can I be excused?"

I ignored my homework and sat outside reading seventeen-year-old Lucas's notes in my Emerson book. He went on a long rant about how churches tried to keep God in a glass box, but that it wasn't the real God of the skies and seas. That God-in-a-box was a cheap imitation.

I wanted to have an encounter with the real God. The wild God. The God who couldn't be captured or franchised or fully explained.

I wanted him to come find me.

I wanted him to send me a dream like the one Wayne had.

Maybe I wanted to look death in the face.

I already made the decision. I wanted to live. I knew that

much.

So I searched for a road.

The ideas were scattered. I couldn't piece them all together. My heart finally settled down and I listened to the wind in the trees and settled under the stars above. The cold front came in around midnight and I reached for my journal.

Then I wrote down the truth.

17

We set up another camping night to celebrate a few milestone events.

First, they freed me from my walking boot. My foot felt stiff but painless. Second, Amado and Malik won the science fair. Third, Wayne's two-week suspension was almost over and he agreed to come back to school. Apparently his dad sat him down and said, "If I could go back in time, I'd do it. I'd go back to where you are and follow through on all the things I said I was going to do. I'd get my dad-gum diploma." This convinced Wayne to stay in school but also reminded him that life was indeed short and adventures needed to be had. He packed up his 4Runner with canned foods and blankets and fishing poles and moved out to Santino's family land to meditate. He made campfires at night and jogged the fence line during the day.

We all needed to lift our spirits.

The past few weeks had been tough.

Everybody found out about the big fight, from Gideon to our parents. Gideon called an emergency meeting and challenged us to be role models for younger students. He gave us a few tips, but the main idea was not to make fools of ourselves in public.

He wrote up an oath that read, "I will be a man of INTEGRITY!" We all signed the oath, except for Wayne, who was living off the land and impossible to reach.

The only other guy in our group who received punishment from the school was Santino. He karate-kicked Todd Michael Avery in the neck. A physical therapist said the blow could have paralyzed him. Santino's dad threatened a lawsuit against the school because he said his son acted in self-defense to preserve his life. They settled on a week of ISS that wouldn't show up in the records. Most everyone was grounded for a week or two. Only Peter showed up to the circle that week since he didn't know anything about the fight. Lucas took him for Vietnamese soup and a trip to the graveyard.

I called Lucas to see if he wanted to come camping with us, but a lady answered who was slurring her words. She sounded crazy, or drunk, or both.

"What's taking you so long?!?"

"Sorry," I said. "I must have the wrong number."

"Are you looking for Lucas?" she asked.

"Yeah. Is he there?"

She paused.

"Are you the peanut butter man?"

"Huh?"

"The peanut butter man."

"I don't think so . . ."

"Then what do you want?"

"I'm one of the seniors from church. Just tell Lucas that Colt called."

"And tell him what?"

"Just let him know I called."

"Wait. You wait one second," she breathed heavily in the receiver. "Are you the peanut butter man?"

"I really don't know what you're talking about."

She hung up. I tried calling back but it went to a generic voicemail. I told the guys about my bizarre conversation on the ride out to Santino's land. I rode shotgun in Peter's minivan, with Amado, Malik, and Charlie in the back.

"Interesting," Malik said. "The mystery deepens."

"What mystery?" Peter asked.

They told him about Lucas possibly having killed someone. They had even added a few new rumors to the mix, each of them more salacious than the last.

"You made all that up," Peter said.

"No I didn't."

"Prove it then."

"That's impossible," Malik said. "Believe me, I've tried. Somebody has gone out of their way to cover up the evidence."

I rolled down the window to feel the wind on my face.

"He's screwing with you, Peter," I said. "They're making things up as they go."

"If that's not true, how come Lucas is in his junior year-book, but not in his senior yearbook? His photo is gone."

"I missed taking my senior photos too."

"But you'll retake them. He missed the whole year. Why?"

"Even if he missed the whole year of school, he could have been sick or lots of things. You're so desperate to find something. Anything. Maybe he didn't feel like taking a picture."

"My mom told me to be careful around him," Malik said. "That he was dangerous. I swear to God she said that."

18

Wayne built a monster bonfire and filled plastic water bottles with gasoline. He pricked the tops of the bottles with his knife so he could squirt gas on the flames at a moment's notice. He grew a nice beard over two weeks and said he hadn't been sleeping very well on account of the howling coyotes. He'd been keeping a dream journal and was running out of room to write.

Something was different about him. He'd changed, if only a little.

When we got there, he showed me some of his dream journal. Every single one of the dreams involved him dying in unexpected ways. He saved a drowning child but then caught an amoeba in the water that dissolved his internal organs. He slipped into a gravel pit and the next day big tractors covered him up with more gravel. A lumberjack cut down a tree and it fell on his head. That kind of stuff. He had a death dream for every night he had been away. No wonder he looked crazier and thinner than normal.

"I already accepted what's going to happen," Wayne said. "You should too."

"You mean I'm going to die from a tree falling on my head?"

"No. But you're going to die just like me. The difference is that you have to wait your turn. The difference is the blink of an eye. It's too small for the cosmos to even notice."

"Cut that out, man."

"No, I'm ready for it. The Coyote King came to me in a dream and said I shouldn't be afraid."

We sat around the fire all evening shooting the breeze. A few guys lay in hammocks reading books, or they went off to explore the woods. While cooking hot dogs, we saw cars coming up the dirt road. Santino stood up and wiped his hands.

"Wh-wh-wh-who's that?"

Wayne bolted upright and ran to brush his teeth.

"I invited some girls over. Clean up. Quick, throw the trash out. Get it together, guys. Don't embarrass me."

"What girls?"

"You don't know them," he said, his mouth full of toothpaste. He ran back and spit in the fire. "When I was jogging the fence line one day in my exile, I met a girl riding on a tractor. She said her family lived on the land next door and then I told her to get a bunch of friends together and come camping with us. I forgot to tell you."

"Damnit, Wayne . . ."

"I'm sorry. I couldn't help it."

Two cars came to a stop, both of them filled with girls.

Wayne greeted the girl he knew with a kiss on the cheek.

"Everybody, this is my good friend . . ."

"Jacy."

"My good friend Jacy. She likes tractors and camping trips with strangers. And of course everybody knows my name is Wayne. Girls, we have hot dogs and potato chips and beverages, and Colt over there was just going to stand up and offer his seat to one of you ladies."

I stood up and waved at them like a dummy. They were hot as hell.

I mean they looked like models in music videos. I don't have any idea how Wayne pulled it off. They went to an expensive private school, and I guess they got tired of dressing in long plaid skirts because they all wore flannels and cutoff jean shorts with holes worn in them. Jacy had a hole worn out over her butt and we saw her tan smooth skin clear as day.

"Isn't it supposed to get cold tonight?" she asked.

"Listen, y'all don't worry about anything," Wayne said. "Set up your tents anywhere you want. We got blankets. We got food. We got a hot fire. We got an ice chest full of drinks. And we got more wood than we could burn, so we're all set."

The girls mingled into the circle around the fire. They found spots on the ground or on tailgates next to the guys. A few of them cooked their own dinner and, like drooling bozos, we just watched them eat. One girl sat on Peter's knee and whispered in his ear. Of all the Wayne stories, this would be the one we talked about the most.

That part's coming.

A girl named Tiffany sat next to me on the tailgate. She had messy dirty-blond hair, summer skin, and shiny cheeks.

"I don't eat hot dogs," she said. "I'm vegetarian."

"I never met a vegetarian."

She grinned and bumped me with her shoulder.

"I do eat fish," she said.

"Well, there's a pond right over there full of fish."

"If you can catch me one I'll eat it."

"Seriously?" I asked.

"Yeah, let's go."

Noa crossed my mind, of course, but there was no harm in showing a girl how to fish. I took a pole and some bait from Wayne's car and we walked through the trees and over the hill toward the pond. Tiffany almost tripped and took my arm. I led her down to the pond and cast the line right where I wanted. She sat on the bank, leaning back on her elbows, watching me work for her dinner. Every once in a while she shot her eyes at me. She took a tube of lip gloss from her back pocket and applied it slowly.

"You have a girlfriend, Colt?"

I admit, I paused.

"Not officially."

"But an unofficial girlfriend?"

"Yeah."

"I bet she's pretty."

"She is."

"I don't think people should have just one boyfriend or girlfriend. It's outdated. We were meant to be with anyone we want to be with."

About that time a catfish nearly yanked the pole out of my hand. I set the hook and started reeling, then handed the pole to Tiffany. She screeched.

"What do I do?"

I put my arms around her and helped her reel in the fish. When we had it on shore she gave me a big hug. Before she separated, she kissed me on the mouth. I laughed a little and backed out of her grip.

"Whoa."

She came in again but I turned my head.

"What's wrong?"

"I just told you I had a girlfriend."

"Not officially, right?"

"Well, but—"

Tiffany walked away from me.

"God, I'm an idiot. I'm so embarrassed."

"Don't be. Really, it's fine."

"It doesn't have to mean anything," she said, clearing the hair from her face. "We'll just pretend like it never happened."

I took her back to the camp and cleaned the fish while she brought me a drink. Since my hands were dirty with fish guts, she put the can to my mouth and helped me drink, laughing when she spilled part of it down my shirt. I fried up the fish over the fire and she ate a couple bites then said she wasn't hungry after all.

I ate the rest. With a full stomach I had a chance to settle down.

I couldn't tell if I was supposed to feel guilty or violated.

Meanwhile I noticed some of the group was missing, including Peter and the girl who had been sitting on his knee. Wayne made out with Jacy in front of everyone. It was shameless. Ortiz and Nate carved sticks into deadly spears. Malik practiced a card trick on Amado. Santino tinkered around with Nate's camera. Over time people wandered back to the fire and cooked s'mores. Peter finally emerged from the woods with his hair tussled. He tried to start a conversation about free will that fell flat.

Just as I was about to set up my tent, Tiffany came over and put her hand on my knee.

"Let's take a walk or something. I need to stretch my legs."

"I think I should hang around here."

I stood up and moseyed over to pretend like I cared about what Ortiz and Nate were doing. Tiffany glared at me from across the fire, working through a bag of potato chips in her lap.

She kept her eyes on me all night—a cold, dead-eyed stare that made me glad I got away from her when I did. I couldn't relax until she fell asleep.

Around three in the morning, when everyone was wrapped up in blankets and the fire was burning low, Wayne nudged me in the ribs. He leaned in close and showed me an extra-large unopened can of beans.

"Just play it cool."

"What?"

"Shh!"

Wayne slid off the tailgate. He crouched at the fire, pretending to shift some logs around. He rolled the can of beans into the center of the coals and made sure no one saw. We were the only ones still awake. Everyone else was snoozing around the fire, either in camping chairs or curled up in the trucks. Wayne crept back over to me and sat down, holding his face in his hands and laughing silently.

"What?"

"Shh."

"Wayne . . ."

"Just wait. Play it cool."

His hand twitched in excitement.

That's when I figured out what was about to happen.

I moved to the back of the truck bed and shielded my eyes. Five or so minutes passed and then KABOOM! It was like someone put a grenade in the middle of the fire. Logs and coals and fire and beans shot everywhere, sending embers up into the cool night sky.

Everyone awoke in terror.

Wayne jumped up and ran circles around the fire with his arms flailing. "What happened?!? What's going on?!?"

Tiffany screamed.

She was *covered* in beans and brown bean juice. *Covered*. The top of that can must have been aimed right at her. She had steaming hot beans in her hair, all over her clothes, and even up her shorts. The bean juice dripped down her neck. The other girls helped her stand and scraped the beans from her hair.

"What . . . the . . . *hell* . . . just happened?!?" She pointed her finger at me, her eyes wide and her teeth bared like a maniac. "You did this! You did this to me!"

"Me? No. I don't know what—"

"I get it, okay! You have a girlfriend!" she screamed. "You're so freaking immature, you jerk!"

Wayne burst into wild laughter. All hell broke loose. She cursed us out and bawled to her friends that she wanted to leave.

Just like that, they gathered up their stuff. Jacy kissed Wayne again then ran to the car. Wayne shrugged and squirted the fire with gasoline to get the flames going again.

Then we blew up every other can we could find.

19

Just because you don't hear the storm on the horizon doesn't mean it's not coming.

Over the next few weeks we all grew really close. The moments we shared started adding up into something special, even though the moments on their own weren't all that remarkable. We stayed too busy to notice what was happening, and now I see what only comes around once in a lifetime. When that magic whirls past your face, you'd better grab as much as you can hold because that may be all you get. Or, as Emerson might say, you'd better look up every once in a while and remember how lucky you are to be alive. Because one day the sky may go dark.

Magic doesn't last forever.

But the magic hung around us for a long time, longer than it does for most. We took one greedy handful after another, thinking nothing this good can ever come to an end.

Every Sunday night that we gathered in the circle, I learned something new about living. And dying.

One night, Lucas showed up in a gold Oldsmobile driven by an old man. I guessed him to be at least seventy-five. I could see a cane in the back seat. Lucas climbed out of the passenger seat and gave a slight wave to the old man as he drove away.

"Is that your grandfather?" Malik asked.

"Your boss?"

"Your parole officer?"

Lucas grinned. He never answered questions about his personal life. Any time we came too close to the truth he turned the question around on us.

Lucas sat on the tailgate next to me. He noticed the journal on my lap.

"Colt. You have anything to share tonight?"

I knew he was going to ask the second he laid eyes on my journal. Even though I was prepared, my heart raced. I had read out loud plenty of times in school. But there was something particularly unsettling about reading my own words. I felt like I was standing butt-naked in the middle of a stadium. I was totally exposed, and I didn't know if what I had to say made any sense.

"Yeah. I can read something I wrote down the other night if that's okay."

"Definitely."

I opened my journal and saw the words I had written the night the cold front blew in. The other guys listened quietly, their eyes fixed on me from across the fire.

"Alright, it's not that great or anything. But here goes . . ."

I took a deep breath and said the truth.

"God is a storm on the horizon, and everybody is looking for shelter. We have names for these shelters, like school and church and friends and sports. We go into these shelters and say we're getting close to God but all we really want to do is hide from the storm. We're scared to see God for who he is. That's why church is the way it is. It's easier to convince yourself there than anywhere else. Well, I'm not playing along. I'm going out into that field and building a campfire and I'm going to wait on the storm to come. I hope I meet him face to face and that storm destroys me. I really do. But if I survive, I'll finally know what I need to know."

Lucas nodded with a slight smile.

"Let's follow that trail tonight. I like where Colt is taking us."

Then he looked up to see Gideon and another man walking briskly toward our group.

Wayne snuffed out his pipe and tossed it into the back of his 4Runner.

Gideon stepped into the circle.

"Hey, guys . . . is someone smoking?"

"It's the fire," Wayne said. "I treated the wood with a . . . *treatment.*"

"Okay. Listen . . . Lucas, you mind if I have a word with you? Guys, Lucas and I need to have a talk. But I'm going to leave you with Tim to finish up tonight. He has the scripture passage and the workbook questions from the weekly curriculum, so you're in good hands."

Gideon motioned for Lucas to follow him.

Tim stepped into the circle. He wore a fuchsia sweater vest and was nearly sixty years old.

Gideon and Lucas walked away from us. I could tell they were arguing. They went into the church offices.

"Catch me up on the conversation," Tim said. He took a crisp sheet of questions out of a folder. "I'd love to hear where you guys are in the curriculum."

"We just finished, actually," Wayne said. "We were going home when you showed up. We already got all the answers right."

"Finished?"

"Yeah. We were leaving when you walked up. You missed the party, amigo."

Wayne motioned for Tim to get off his tailgate and then he slammed it shut. Wayne got into his car, cranked up the music, and drove off without another word.

The rest of us followed.

20

Knock, knock, knock.

I opened my bedroom window and found Wayne standing there in the cold. It was after midnight on Christmas Eve.

"Lucas is back. He wants us all to get together, right now. Let's ride."

I grabbed some shoes and closed the window softly behind me.

This was big news.

We hadn't seen or heard from Lucas since the night Gideon took him away from the circle, which was almost a month before. We finally discovered what the fuss was all about. Apparently, some of the parents in the church had been complaining that we weren't being given a "biblical education" in our small group, and so Gideon decided to replace Lucas with Tim. We narrowed the chief complainer down pretty quickly to Peter's mom.

When we confronted Peter about it, he admitted his mom had been drilling him for weeks about the circle. He had done his best not to say anything that might compromise us, but he had eventually told her about the graveyard, the bridge, and even Lucas wanting us to ask questions instead of being spoon-fed answers.

In response to Lucas's excommunication, Wayne wrote a letter to Gideon warning that if Lucas wasn't reinstated as our small group leader, then he would take out an ad in the Sunday paper to publicly renounce his faith. We piled into Peter's minivan and delivered the letter to Gideon's home mailbox and sped off before sunrise.

Evidently, the letter had made an impact.

I jumped in the car with Wayne and he drove to the cemetery. When we pulled up, all the other guys were already gathered in the back field. They stood in silence, shadows under the half moon.

As we walked toward them, Lucas held a finger up to his lips, as if to request silence.

We found our spots with the others. On the ground beside Lucas was a lump of something covered by a blanket.

He bent down and cast the blanket aside to reveal a pile of samurai swords, sheathed in black plastic with handles of criss-crossed gold thread. He picked one up and approached Santino, who stood the closest.

"For the last few weeks, I have been traveling through Southeast Asia on a soul odyssey," Lucas said. "I bought these swords in a village outside of Chiang Mai in Thailand. May these swords remind you that horizons are not boundaries. That the world is waiting for you, but you must fight for your freedom. For your dreams. For your convictions."

Lucas bent down on one knee and presented the sword to Santino. Santino bent down with him.

"Will you fight with everything you have?"

"I will," Santino said.

"Go. Be courageous and true."

One by one, Lucas worked down the line asking the same question to each of us. Will you fight with everything you have? I was at the end of the line and had more time to consider the question than everyone else. By the time he came to me I was ready to answer. I bent down on one knee and he offered the sword to me.

"Will you fight with everything you have?"

"I will."

"Go. Be courageous and true."

The sword felt like a lightning bolt in my hands.

21

The second semester started and I continued tutoring Harold.

He told me all he did over Christmas break was eat pizza and drink off-brand cola in the basement. Apparently he and Presley kept an arsenal of video games and DVDs and never went outside unless the pizza man rang the doorbell. On $5 pizza night they ordered a week's worth. They switched between *Mortal Kombat* and a game with mercenaries killing each other on a distant planet. Whenever Presley died on the digital battlefield, he kicked holes in the wood paneling and spit on Harold. To his credit, Harold finally passed the computer test for *The Outsiders*. The victory earned him enough points for a sack of plastic green army men. He trashed the prize and said he wasn't a kid anymore, but a 'full-grown man'.

So I drove him to the bookstore to pick out his next challenge.

Noa waited for us outside the front doors.

"Hey, Noa. Sorry I'm tagging along," Harold said. "If you two need some privacy, just let me know."

She glanced at me, then back down at him.

"Harold. Glad you could join us."

Harold went for the middle grade section while me and

Noa strolled toward the back. I made sure he went past the romance novels. He peeked at a cover or two but kept a steady pace.

Noa dusted her finger along the spines, dressed in navy warm-up pants and a jacket with a furry hood.

"So what are we in the market for today?" she asked. "Adventure? Mystery? A love story?"

"Maybe I want something with all of it."

"That's going to be hard to find."

"Well, I believe in us. I think we can do it."

We walked through the aisles and our hands brushed together.

"Now that you're a proud sword owner, you should get a book on sword fighting."

She had found the sword in the back of my truck and I told her about what happened in the graveyard. Ever since then, it had been a running joke for her, but she also understood why it was so important to me.

"I didn't tell you, but I wrote the book on sword fighting," I said. "I already know everything there is to know."

"Is that right?"

"That's right. I'm something of an expert."

"Wow. Well, I feel really honored to be in your presence right now."

"Please. At the end of the day, I'm just a normal person who is an expert swordsman. You don't have to treat me any differently."

"Don't worry. I won't."

She looked past me and her smile faded. She motioned for me to turn around.

James sat on the ground leafing through a book. He hadn't seen me yet. He looked like a completely different person, twenty pounds lighter with a buzzed head. Ever since the big fight, James had been oddly quiet. He kept his head down at school, talked to no one in the halls, and worked in silence. People worried Wayne had given him brain damage.

"Come on," I said. "Let's get out of here."

Noa stopped me with a hand on my chest.

"You need to go over and say something."

"Noa . . ."

She gave me a look that said I had no choice. She patted my chest then pushed me toward him.

"Fine."

"I'll keep an eye on Harold."

I walked over and slid down the wall next to him. We sat in silence for a minute.

"It's been a while," James said, still reading. "How you been?"

"Pretty good. How about you?"

"I'm all right. They put my tooth back."

He opened his mouth to show me. Everything was good as new.

"This book is about a guy who rides a train from England all the way to India and then Russia and all the way back home. Crazy guy. He almost dies a few times."

"I didn't know you liked books."

"I didn't know you liked books."

"Maybe there's a lot we don't know about each other," I said.

"I saw you with Noa. Y'all serious now?"

"Yeah I guess," I said. "Depends on what you mean by serious."

"She's pretty cool. Hey man. I'm sorry."

He shut the book and extended a hand for me to shake.

"This whole year. It just . . . it started off wrong, that's all."

I shook his hand.

"Yeah. Me too. I didn't want any of this."

"I think I watched too many movies about senior year and . . . I don't know. We acted like freaking idiots and got pulled apart. Stupid. I keep wishing we could go back to the very first day and just chill. Maybe go out to your grandparents' place and ride go-karts or throw the ball around or something. You pick a college yet?"

"Not yet," I said. "I'm waiting to hear back."

"Apply anywhere cool?"

"Paris."

He smirked. "No kidding. Would you really go all the way over there?"

"I don't think I'll get in."

"What about Noa?"

"What about her?"

"Y'all going to break up or try to go long distance?"

Down the row of shelves I saw Noa joking with Harold. She took a book off the shelf and showed him the back cover, giving him a hard sell. To be honest, I hadn't thought much about what would happen with Noa.

"We haven't talked about it yet."

"I can see it, man," he said. "The two of you. When I first heard, I thought you were just trying to be different but I can see it. You fit together."

"How are the other guys?"

"I don't know. I've been laying low, man. Real low," James said.

"The tooth?"

"The tooth. And not a single one of those guys came by to

see me. Not one. It's like you got too many friends until it gets tough, then you're on your own. I didn't know it would be like that."

"Yeah."

"You just went and got new friends."

"You holding that against me?"

"No. I'm jealous," James said. "That's the honest truth, Colt. I hated you because you beat me to it. Doing something different."

"There's still time," I said.

"For what?"

"Come to the circle."

"And have that psycho Wayne knock out my teeth and shoot me with his stun gun? No thanks."

"I'm serious."

"Colt, at least two of those guys want to kill me. They said so to my face."

"They got it out of their system. Part of the whole deal is to move forward, not backwards. To see the big picture."

"Right."

He shook his head and opened the book.

"Sunday night," I reminded him. "Seven o'clock. Bring a journal and a pen."

Craig Cunningham

22

The next Sunday night, we found Lucas sitting on the back steps of the church smoking his pipe. He sent us upstairs and encouraged us not to cause any trouble if we still wanted to be able to meet in the parking lot. The circle was officially on thin ice.

As soon as we arrived on the second floor, Gideon walked up on stage.

"Hey, everyone. Welcome back. I hope you had a good winter break. We have an exciting new program for this semester." Gideon found all of us senior guys gathered in the back corner. "And I know that we'll all be sticking to the curriculum."

Amado gave him a double thumbs-up.

That's when I saw James standing alone on the other side of the room. He held a journal and a pen. He nodded at me. The other guys saw him too. Wayne approached me, turning his back to James.

"Colt, tell me you don't see James over there."

"So what?"

"You brought him here?"

"I didn't bring him here. He came by himself."

"Tell him the group is full or something."

"Don't be mean."

"Me be mean? In case you forgot, this guy cracked eggs on my music collection. He told everyone in the whole school my dong was blue. Colt, this is the king of all jerk-offs."

"Listen to yourself."

"I know what I'm saying. We have a good thing going. He's going to screw it all up."

Wayne and the other guys went down the stairs to the parking lot, and I stayed behind. Noa watched me approach James. She raised her eyebrows at me with a smile then joined her group of girls.

"You made it," I said to James.

"Listen, bro, if this is too weird, I'm going to leave. It's not really my scene, anyways."

"It's cool. Don't worry about it."

"You sure?" he asked.

"Yeah, come on. At least try it once."

"What'd Wayne just say to you?"

"He said he's excited you're here."

"Yeah. I bet."

I led James down the stairs and into the parking lot. Up ahead, everyone's trucks were already circled around the fire. I forgot to tell James we met outside in the elements, even in the dead of winter. I bet he was freezing in his long-sleeve t-shirt. We walked into the circle and took a seat on my tailgate. Everybody stayed silent, watching James. Lucas noticed the tension but moved past it.

"Hey, man," Lucas said. "What's your name?"

"I'm James."

Lucas shook his hand.

"I'm Lucas. Glad you're here. You know these guys?"

"Uh, yeah. Most of them."

"Then you're with friends."

James shivered and crossed his arms when a bitter wind bounced between us.

Wayne lit his pipe. He made a funny noise, like he was holding back laughter at a joke no one else heard. With a Mexican blanket wrapped around his shoulders, he looked up to the sky just about the time it started snowing.

He tossed the blanket to James.

"Here I am tumbling at a hundred miles an hour toward the end of my life, and trying to go backwards won't do much good now," Wayne said. "I can't go in reverse."

"Thanks," James said, a little confused.

Lucas stood over the flames of the barrel.

"Everything is meaningless," he recited from Ecclesiastes. "Generations come and generations go, but the earth remains forever."

James pulled the blanket tight.

23

I collapsed on the couch, exhausted from tutoring Harold. That's when I heard a familiar voice in the kitchen talking with my mom.

Noa stuck her head into the living room.

"Oh, hey Colt. By the way, your mom invited me to dinner. We're having barbecue chicken. Yum."

They had made the plans without me knowing.

Her and my mom talked in the kitchen for a while about the latest news from school while I sat on the couch staring at the TV that wasn't on. My dad and little brother were outside grilling chicken and throwing the football. I had a pit in my stomach because a few of my college application letters came back. I was officially accepted to five schools, none of them in Texas. I hadn't even told my family, much less Noa. She had already earned a full ride to play music at UNT.

Noa plopped on the couch beside me.

"What's up?"

"Hey."

"You just watching the wall?"

"Want to go in my room and make out?"

She glanced toward the kitchen where my mom chopped carrots for the salad, then back at me.

"Definitely," she said.

We crept down the hall.

"Doors open!" my mom shouted. "No closed doors!"

"I'm just showing her a book!" I called back.

We walked into my room and fell on the bed making out. No matter how many times we had kissed, it never seemed to get old.

"Easy," she said. "I don't want red-face before dinner."

I heard my mom walking down the hall and picked up a book from underneath my bed. I flipped it to the middle.

". . . and the author says here that deep in the mystical mountains of Colorado . . ."

My mom peeked into the room as she passed with an armful of clean laundry. On her way back she told us to come to the table. My little brother ate shirtless since the chicken had barbecue sauce.

"So, Noa. What do you think of this sacred circle stuff the boys are so into these days?"

"It's fun."

"I think so too. Swords and poetry and adventures."

Mom winked at me.

"Yeah, Lucas has been pretty awesome for the guys," Noa said.

My mom's smile faded a little as she nodded.

"These rolls, Noa, are just . . . wonderful. I'm going to have another one even though I shouldn't. Mmm. So good."

"Why'd you look like that?" I asked.

"Like what?"

"When Noa said Lucas was doing a good job with us, you made a funny look."

"Did I?" Mom asked.

"Yeah."

"Well, I'm just glad to hear that he's back on track."

"What do you mean back on track?"

"I don't know. He's just . . . been through a lot. And he's sort of a wanderer. Is that what you would say, honey?"

My dad nodded. "I think that's fair to say. A wanderer. A really talented guy. I like him."

"Anyway, I think he's great for you and the boys. Really, I do. In fact I'm going to write him a letter telling him so."

"Please don't."

"I won't embarrass you. I just want to show my appreciation. You reminded me."

After dinner, me and Noa went out on the back porch despite my mom saying it was too cold. I turned off the porch lights and put on some music. We cozied up on the patio furniture.

"I like your family," Noa said. "They're sweet."

"Yeah. They're weird but I guess everybody's family is weird."

"I don't think they're weird."

"Keep coming over and you'll see."

I wanted to tell her about the college letters. But if I did, it would open the door to a conversation I wasn't quite ready to have. I still didn't know what I wanted. Some days I wanted to go far away and lose myself in a brand-new experience, while other days I wanted to be with her forever. Some days I wanted to be lonely on the other side of the world, and other days I thought that was a stupid thing to want. I figured time would make the decision for me.

"So what's the story with Lucas?" Noa asked.

"I honestly don't know."

"Sounds like he went through a hard time or something."

"I wouldn't count on anything my mom says. Half of what she hears is wrong."

I thought about mentioning Emerson's *Essays*, and how I had been going through Lucas's notes in the margins. I couldn't quite pin down exactly what had happened to him. But I knew, without a shadow of a doubt, that something had happened that year which drastically changed his life. And whatever it was had hurt other people, too.

"Malik has been trying to figure him out for months," I said. "We only know that there's some kind of mystery about where he spent the last seven years. Malik has all kinds of theories, like Lucas killed someone, or he won the lottery, or he crashed a bus into an elementary school or something."

"What? That's horrible."

"I know. It's stupid."

"Why don't you just ask Lucas?"

"You can't just ask this guy a question. He's like the wind. You can't get a hold of him no matter how hard you try. You ask him a question, and he turns it around on you somehow. Or he speeds off into the darkness. Or he gazes out at the horizon and whispers a quote to himself. I hardly know anything about him except his name."

"Have you tried just . . . asking him?"

"No, not directly."

She groaned. "Boys can be so stupid."

I picked her up off the couch and carried her to the swimming pool. I held her over the water. She squirmed around to be set free.

"Stop! Put me down. Colt. I'm dead serious."

"You want me to put you down right here?"

"Not here. Back there. Colt . . . you seriously don't want to do this. It's freezing!"

"I'm just a stupid boy."

"Listen. If you drop me in this water, I will . . ."

"What?"

She put a finger in my face.

"I will be very mad at you."

I paused for a moment.

"I can deal with that."

I jumped in with her.

24

As a way to make up for our lost weeks in the circle, Lucas invited us to a campout. He said that, in the spirit of bonding, one night of camping was worth a dozen nights of parking lot discussions.

We carpooled down toward the east side of town and found Lucas's house at the end of a cul-de-sac. The place was sort of run down, with paint chipping off the exterior walls. In the driveway, a homeless man leaned against a toppled-over shopping cart and sang the national anthem with his hand over his heart. The front door was wide open. We all went inside with Peter huddled in between us for protection. James held up the rear. He hadn't said much since joining the circle but at the same time he hadn't missed a moment with us.

We paused in the entryway.

A few strange people lounged around the living room reading magazines, watching television, fiddling around with board games. A skinny guy shouted into the telephone that he needed a ride to Dallas. One old woman slept on the couch. In the kitchen I saw a man lick a butter knife and put it back in the drawer.

Charlie turned around. "I think this is a crack house. We

better bolt!"

"You looking for Lucas?"

The woman on the couch sat up and brushed back her frizzy hair with her hand. She was missing an eye. Amado gasped.

"Yes."

"Which one of you is the peanut butter man?" She glared at us, waiting on an answer.

"I am." I stepped forward. "I'm the peanut butter man."

The other guys had no idea what I meant, but she seemed appeased.

She smiled.

"He's in the back. Right through this hall. Don't steal anything."

"Lucas lives here? Like this tall. Dark hair. A little older than us?"

"That's the man." She rolled over and clicked the remote to the Weather Channel.

Wayne led the charge down the dark hallway and knocked on the door. Lucas opened it.

"Oh, thank God," Wayne said.

"You found it. Come in. What's up, guys?"

We scuttled into his room and shut the door behind us.

"I'm finishing something up, so you can just chill for a minute," Lucas said.

We spread throughout the room in silence. Incense burned on top of the dresser. The room was crowded with relics from worldwide travels, paintings of the Himalayas, weapons like the swords he gave us in the graveyard. A mattress lay on the floor, covered in fur blankets. Stacked around the bed were hundreds and hundreds of books. Peter took a seat on a stack of books and crossed his legs.

"You know there's three or four homeless people in your living room, right?" Wayne asked.

"Yeah," Lucas said.

"This one-eyed lady is laying on your couch watching the Weather Channel."

"Yeah. That's Wanda."

"She's a cyclops."

"Yeah."

Lucas sat at his desk typing on a computer. We all looked at each other in disbelief.

"Just making sure you knew."

"Hang on, guys. Give me a minute."

Covering every square inch of wall space were movie posters — *E.T.*, *Legends of the Fall*, *Braveheart*, *Dead Poets Society*, and more.

"Is this like a halfway house or something?"

Malik perked up at the possibility. He filed every odd detail about Lucas into his imagination.

"No, man. I own this place. It's my house."

"They live here too?"

"No."

"They just come in and watch TV?"

"Sometimes. The door is always open."

"What if somebody sneaks in and cuts your throat while you're sleeping?"

"What would someone gain by doing that?"

"Your wallet. Your computer."

He ignored us and kept typing.

Wayne sat down next to me with a photo album. We thumbed through the pictures taken all over the world, from China to Los

Angeles. Tucked in some of the picture sleeves were scraps of paper covered in quotes or inspirational thoughts attached to the memories of each place. Seeing the handwriting, I had no doubts Lucas was the one who wrote in my copy of Emerson's *Essays*. One of the photos was Lucas with a beautiful teenage girl when he was about our age. It seemed like they went to the prom together. I felt guilty nosing around, but I wanted to know more about the guy we had been following around for half a year.

"Alright, fellas. Come look at this."

We crowded around the desk to see his computer. Lucas had assembled all of our journal writings from the circle into a file for a book. Each one of us guys had a chapter of our own. Lucas even made a front cover with a photo of us lifting our swords up to the moon in the empty field at the back of the graveyard.

"At the end of the year I'm going to print these up for you guys to keep. Or pass out to your families, or sell them, or whatever you want. It will be a book, this big."

"Badass! We'll all be published writers!" Wayne shouted.

"My d-d-d-ad owns part of a publishing company," Santino said. "I bet we could get them p-p-printed for free."

"Everything has a way of working out. It always does." Lucas turned to us. "Alright. Let's head out."

We piled into the back of his truck with our camping gear, and he drove us out to some land we'd never been to before. We settled under a big oak tree beside the river. Lucas made a ring out of rocks and built a campfire. Wayne brought out a small ice chest filled with hot dogs and stuff for s'mores.

At dark, we settled into a circle around the fire.

I scanned the skies but the stars weren't out yet.

"Hey, Lucas, have you ever been arrested?" Malik asked out of nowhere.

He shot his eyes over at Amado.

Lucas took a deep breath.

"Once. For jumping trains. Wow. I just noticed the moon." Lucas pointed up at the full moon dripping through the branches above our heads. "One day, traveling into outer space will be just as normal as traveling down the highway. Think about it. It's inevitable. We'll have civilizations on Mars. Maybe one of you guys will be the first Governor of Mars."

Malik leaned against the trunk of the tree, exasperated for answers.

"I always wanted to be an astronaut," Amado said.

"Then be one," Lucas said.

"It's not that easy. I went to space camp for a few years down at NASA and it's a one in a million shot to be a real astronaut."

"Then be the one in a million."

"Right."

"I'm serious. Someone is going to be the one astronaut in a million."

Amado nodded. "Maybe."

"All of you guys have the potential to do whatever you want in this life," Lucas said. "You can fly a spaceship or go see the pyramids in Egypt. Anything. But you have to make it happen for yourself. You can't just want it."

The circle fell silent for a moment.

"What about you, James?" Lucas asked.

James lay on his back, looking up through the trees at the moon. He sat up.

"What about me?"

"What's your one in a million?"

"Oh. I don't know. I haven't thought about it really."

He was lying. I knew he was. He breathed faster and faster, but Lucas didn't notice.

"Just think about this," Lucas continued. "How many old men, wheezing for their final breaths, would give *anything* to be eighteen again? You have your whole life before you."

Wayne cleared his throat. "I want to dance with a pretty girl . . ."

". . . In Mexico," we all said.

"But that's just the beginning," Wayne said. He stood up. "I'm also going to sail a ship around the world and dive into the deepest part of the ocean. I'm going to ride a camel from one end of the Sahara Desert to the other. I'm going to sit down across from the wisest men in the world and ask for their best advice. I'm going to sleep in a teepee and be blessed by a medicine man. I'm going to howl with wolves. I'm going to see all the wonders of the world and I'm going to get in a hot air balloon and float over the Great Wall of China. I'm going to build a house with my bare hands and race a car at the Daytona racetrack. I'm going to ride a horse into the mountains and camp out for six months. I'm going to catch a fish in the rivers of Montana. But first, I have to dance with a pretty girl in Mexico."

None of us doubted Wayne.

He could have kept going with a hundred ideas while all of us struggled for a single dream worth pursuing. I never thought that far ahead. I could only see a few inches in front of my face while Wayne saw his whole life from this moment until the last, and from the last moment back toward this one. If you could go all the way to the end and look backwards, the decisions became much easier. Nobody wants to look backwards from the last breath and see a life without purpose. Nobody wants to see all the opportunities they passed up. Nobody wants to wish they could be eighteen again because they missed the train the first time around.

I tried to think of myself as an old man with one more breath in my lungs.

What would make it all worthwhile?

"I want to be a new person," James said abruptly. He was almost shaking. "Brand new. I hate who I am."

We all fell silent. Of all the people who might hate themselves, James seemed the least likely candidate.

"I haven't told anybody about this. But I'll just say it. I'm tired of keeping things in." He stood up in the middle of the circle of guys. Firelight swarmed in his eyes. "I tried to kill myself. On Christmas Eve night. I took a bunch of pills I found in my mom's cabinet and wanted them to kill me. But it didn't work. I just got really sick. They found me on the ground and we spent Christmas Day and New Year's in the hospital. I was pissed. I wanted it to work. I wanted to die. And I was planning on trying again, then I ran into Colt and figured I'd give this group a shot. So I don't know what you think of me. I know I've been a dick for a long time. Nobody knows that better than me. I just want to be a new person."

25

At dawn the next morning, we woke up with Lucas standing over us holding a sack of kolaches.

"Morning, guys! How'd you sleep?"

We groaned. Just four hours earlier we had been roaring like maniacs around the fire.

"Climb into the back of the truck. I want to show you something."

We made our way over to the truck and got in the bed. Wayne dug into the sack of kolaches and began handing them out.

"James, ride up front with me," Lucas called.

James rode shotgun and the rest of us huddled in the back.

We got going down a dirt road and Peter sat up with the sun hitting him in the face.

"Where are we going now?"

"I don't know," Wayne said. "Could be anywhere. *Anywhere*, Pete!"

Peter shook his head in disbelief, like his life was spinning out of control.

Wayne laughed and told us to eat up, saying we would need strength for whatever adventure awaited.

Through the back windshield of the truck I could see James and Lucas deep in conversation. We spent plenty of time in the circle talking about how death could sneak up on you at any minute. But we never talked about the possibility of orchestrating your own death, at least not in a physical sense. All of a sudden, someone I had known my whole life felt like a total stranger. I probably seemed the same way to him when I started going to the circle. The James I knew would never in a million years consider killing himself. Never. He had funny friends and easy girls and access to all the good things in life. Maybe the 'good things' turned out to be meaningless, just like it said in Ecclesiastes.

We drove for a few more minutes across the land until Lucas came to a stop.

He got out of the truck and crowed at the sky.

Then, he took off his shirt and pants and jogged into the woods wearing only navy boxer briefs. Nobody knew what on earth was happening.

"I guess we should follow him?"

We undressed down to our underwear, too.

Lucas whistled for us from the distance.

A hundred yards into the woods we found him standing on the edge of a limestone cliff, looking down into a murky pool fed by a waterfall.

"*Whoa.*"

"What is this place?"

"This is Tonkawa Falls," Lucas said. "The old guy who you thought was my parole officer owns this land. So we can jump all we want. Who's going first?"

We edged toward the cliff and looked down.

Twenty feet may not sound like much, but when you're

twenty feet off the ground facing the prospect of jumping into unfamiliar water it puts a stone in your throat.

"How deep is it?"

"Plenty deep," Lucas said. "I already checked the water this morning. It's at least twelve feet deep right there. Trust me."

Peter stood at the front of the pack.

"Go for it, Pete."

"I'm not jumping. I just want to see."

"Come on!"

"No. I don't like cold water. Somebody else can go."

He tried to push his way to the back of the group but we held him at the front.

"How about this . . ." Wayne said. "You jump, and I'll pierce my nipples. Both of them. I'll put big gold rings in there."

"You wouldn't actually do it."

"I swear I would. Have I ever lied to you?"

"Not to me directly, but you've lied to lots of other people."

"Why would you offer that?" Nate asked. "It's like you just want an excuse to pierce your nipples."

"I don't care what it is. I'll get a tattoo or go run around naked at the mall or anything at all. I just want to see Peter jump. I like watching people go crazy!"

"Back up." James moved through the group and extended his hand to Peter. "We'll jump at the same time."

"You'll do it with me?"

"Yep."

Peter hesitantly shook his hand.

James glanced back at Lucas. "Carpe diem, right?"

"Carpe diem," Lucas replied.

Peter put his toes to the edge of the cliff. He handed his

dad's dog tags to me for safekeeping. We counted down from three and Peter and James leapt off the cliff with a barbaric yawp.

26

Time blew past us with disregard, and the golden promise of senior year grew shorter and shorter. I needed to make some decisions about my life—Noa, college, the big picture of what kind of man I might set out to become. All I knew for certain was the road I had been walking for so many years would no longer exist in a few short months.

I needed a new road.

A better one.

One I could call my own.

After first period I stood at my locker sorting through college acceptance letters.

I was still waiting on a few responses, but I had plenty of options. Noa knew we needed to talk about our relationship as boyfriend and girlfriend. She hated that I was so noncommittal about next year, which made her think something was wrong with us being together. Every time she brought up college, I changed the subject.

Wayne punched the locker next to me.

"Whoa. What's wrong?"

He pressed his back to the lockers and slid to the floor. He handed me a report card. I unfolded the paper and saw everything from C to F.

"There's a few Cs," I pointed out. "And your conduct is improving, for the most part. That's good."

"We've got one last report card," he said. "If I get one more D, they said I would flunk and have to do this year all over again. We both know that's not happening. I'll be on the first airplane to Okinawa before I spend another year in this hole."

Villarreal strolled past and pointed at Wayne.

"Off the floor, chump. I pay good money to have these floors waxed. I don't need your dirty rear end scuffing them up."

Wayne casually flipped him off.

Villarreal stopped in his tracks.

"A couple of hotshots, huh?" he said, then stormed over to us. "Big dogs begging to be let out of the kennel."

He snatched the report card out of my hands and read through it with a smile.

"How about that?"

Wayne stood up so they were nose to nose.

"How about what?"

They looked like two people about to kiss, or kill each other. A few students slowed down to see what might happen. Wayne tilted his chin up so he could stare down on Villarreal.

"I know who you are, Wayne."

"You don't know anything about me."

"You're a nobody. A loser. A do-over."

Villarreal offered the report card back to Wayne. When Wayne reached out, Villarreal let it drop to the floor.

"Whoops. My bad."

He strolled off whistling and combing his hair. Somebody

threw a paper airplane off the second-floor balcony that hit Villarreal in the neck. He bolted up the stairs to chase them down.

"I can't do it, Colt. If I'm going to flunk out of here, I might as well give myself a head start and pack up the car and go now. I have to wake up every day at six to be here, and I could be waking up every day at six to watch the sun rise on the ocean. Think about that. I give eight hours a day to this place. If I gave the same eight hours a day to a small business, I could be a millionaire in a year. I'd invite you and Noa to come and sunbathe on my yacht."

"Don't quit."

"I'm serious. I read about all these billionaires who quit school. I'm actually a smart guy, you know. I can figure out ways to make money without knowing what year George Washington sent a letter to the king of France. This place is only holding me back."

He felt low the rest of the day, so low in fact that he ate in the lunchroom instead of on his tailgate listening to Mexican radio. James and Noa sat with us at the corner table.

We told her about Tonkawa Falls.

"Did you jump too, Colt?"

"Yeah. We all did. We're going back next weekend if you want to come. We should get a big group together."

About then, Presley Thomas walked past our table, carrying his lunch cooler and listening to loud music on his headphones. He wore baggy black jeans and a tour t-shirt for some band called Living Nightmare. James watched Presley go to the opposite side of the lunchroom and sit on a massive windowsill by himself. He unpacked two slices of cheese pizza and stared out the window. James reached into his backpack and took out a list of names, with half of them crossed off, including Wayne's. He moved his finger down the list until he found Presley's name, then marked it off.

"Good luck," I said.

"Thanks."

James went to join Presley in the windowsill. We watched as James tapped Presley on the shoulder then began a conversation.

"What's he doing?" Noa asked.

"Starting over," I said.

27

Harold made some big improvements in his reading comprehension, mostly because he fell in love with a comic book series called *SkatterBrain* about a kid who looked exactly like him who served as a mediator between world leaders and aliens. Harold took out a one-hundred-dollar loan from his mom to buy all the editions he could get his hands on. He'd read all of them ten or twenty times. With that kind of devotion he was able to pick out plot devices and character development with no difficulty at all. He aced a couple of the reading comprehension computer tests without even reading the books.

At our next meeting he showed up wearing polarized sunglasses.

"I don't think I need you anymore," Harold said.

"Your teachers disagree."

"But they're dumb."

"You can take your glasses off now. There's no sun in here."

"Oh these . . ." He lifted them onto his head. "Forgot I was wearing them. Won these with my reading points. On the street they're worth a hundred dollars."

"No they aren't."

"I saw the same glasses selling on the internet for a hundred and fifty dollars."

"What are you trying to prove?"

"Don't have to prove that I'm ballin'." He reached into his backpack and took out a deck of magician's playing cards. "Hey, how's Noa?"

"Good."

"Work out the long-distance relationship thing or are you still dragging your feet?"

"I don't know what we're going to do yet, but you definitely won't be the first person I tell."

"I think you should get married."

"Oh yeah?"

"That way she won't be able to date other guys while you're away at college."

The teacher glanced over. I waved that everything was okay.

"You don't know what you're talking about. Read your book."

He flipped a few pages without reading the words, clearly distracted by thoughts of me and Noa.

"Colt. You have to know that ballers like me will chase after her if you're a thousand miles away. I'm not that much younger than her, biologically speaking. It's the law of nature. I'm just saying if it was me, I'd lock her up with a ring. You can always take it back if things don't work out. But, hey, do whatever you want. It's your life."

He made a pretty good point.

"Read your book and stop talking." I tapped the cover.

After the tutoring session, we sat on the steps outside the school waiting for Harold's mom. She worked late and never arrived on time.

A little black Suzuki came to a stop, rattling with heavy metal music.

"Oh God," Harold said. "It's my nutzo brother."

He walked down the steps to the car. I nodded a hello to Presley, who opened his door and stood facing me, talking over the top of the car. He lit a cigarette and put the lighter on the car.

"Hey, Presley."

"Hey, man."

"I didn't realize Harold was your brother until we put it all together," I said.

"Yeah. Sorry if he's an idiot."

Harold rolled his eyes.

"No, we have a good time."

"How's the foot?" Presley asked. "You broke it or something right?"

"Last fall, yeah. It's good now."

"Yeah. Sorry I don't keep up with every little thing, man."

"You going to college next year?"

"No. I'm getting away. Way the hell away."

He blew smoke out the corner of his mouth. I could tell he had something to say, no doubt about James's conversation at lunch. Like many outcasts, he hated James, and for good reason. Freshman year, James wrote a sexy love letter to one of the most popular senior girls, signed by Presley Thomas, Locker #7012. She showed the letter to her boyfriend, who gathered a posse of his wrestling teammates and met Presley at the locker between classes. They slapped his books to the floor and roughed him up. James watched from afar. The wrestlers attacked Presley at random the whole year. He changed his bus route twice. Sometimes he'd be walking down the hall minding his business and a crowd would surround him to rip down his pants or call him a queer or anything else you can imagine. He came back sophomore year wearing all black and threatened to murder whoever messed with him.

For whatever reason, we always got along just fine.

"Alright. Well tell your mom Harold needs to read fifteen pages tonight. The book is in his bag."

"Yeah. I'll tell her. Hey, listen. What was that about today with James?" he asked.

"I think he's trying to make things right with people."

"Is he screwing with me? Be honest."

"No. I really don't think he's screwing with you."

"He told me he tried to kill himself on Christmas Eve. That's crazy."

"Yeah."

"And about some circle group or something."

"Yeah."

Presley took a long drag then put out the cigarette on the car. He flicked the butt into the bushes.

"You think I could maybe come?"

28

We were sitting on the back porch at my house when Wayne walked through the gate rolling a cooler behind him.

"Tacos. Two dozen of them, and all different kinds. Eat up, chumps."

"What's the expiration date?"

"I don't know. They're all out of date, so who cares."

"There's a big difference between a day and a month."

"Those dates are just so the health inspectors don't cause any trouble."

He set the cooler in the middle of us. A few guys reluctantly grabbed tacos. We had all agreed to attend the upcoming senior party hosted at a big three-story house that backed up to Harris Creek, and so the guys had all met at my house to ride together. The host of the party, Cameron Wakefield, intended to make it the most unforgettable senior party of all time. He printed flyers and put them on cars in the parking lot. He lobbied all of the different groups to make an appearance. To the swim team, he promised access to the pool. To the drunks, he confirmed a king's variety of liquor and beer. To the nerds, he assured an entire room readied with board games and soda. To the church kids, he guaranteed the presence of his devout parents.

"Oh gross." James spit his taco on the pavement. My dog sniffed it then walked away.

"They aren't *that* bad."

"Is this meat?"

"It tastes like an old banana."

"You guys could be grateful instead of complaining about free food. Fine, pay five bucks for a measly hamburger."

Wayne always sought out ways to save money and took offense at reckless spenders. He told me once that more people ought to live in tents, and said you could still have a television and access to showers. He rented a documentary about a group of people who worked full-time jobs and made six figure salaries but were still classified as homeless. The movement inspired him. Any time he pocketed an extra dollar or two he talked about contributing to 'the fund'. No one knew what he meant. Ortiz asked if he was also an investor in growth-stock mutual funds. Wayne said no, then changed his answer to 'of course'.

"How we going to ride?"

We had eight guys with us: me, Ortiz, Amado, Malik, Wayne, James, Santino, and Nate. But if you counted Peter, our circle was up to nine. We invited him to join us but he said his family rented a movie and he needed to be there to work the DVD player.

"You can all fit in the back of my truck," I said.

"Shotgun."

"Shotgun. No!"

"All right. Let's jet."

"Oh yeah, I can't believe I almost forgot." Malik held out his hands for us to brace ourselves. "I found out about Lucas.

Everything. And it's all certified information. I even called up Gideon and asked him about it, and he confirmed the story. The mystery is solved, no thanks to you guys."

"What is it?!"

"Let me guess," I said. "He didn't kill anyone."

"Actually . . . he did," Malik said. I felt a pit in my stomach. "Just before his senior year started, he was driving with his friend one night coming back from a hiking trip and fell asleep at the wheel. They ran off the road and flipped into a ditch. His best friend died, but Lucas walked away without a scratch."

We sat in stunned silence. I couldn't imagine dealing with that kind of guilt. How could anyone move on from something like that?

"But there's more to the story. A lot more," Malik said. "A few weeks later, he ran away from home."

"What do you mean, ran away from home?"

"Apparently, the week before his senior year started, his mom went into his room one morning and he was gone. He took off overnight. And there was no trace of where he went, almost like aliens abducted him. Just . . . *gone*. His family and friends searched the town for days but couldn't find any leads. His girlfriend was crushed because she thought they were all in love and going to get married. He left everything behind. Toothbrush. Underwear. Cash. He even left his car. They sent out search teams all over the state to find him and eventually gave him up for dead. He didn't write a letter to his family or friends or anything. They thought maybe he jumped off a bridge or something because of the guilt from his friend dying in the car accident."

"So what happened?"

"Well, they questioned this old professor named Hue Schrader. They thought he might know something. Apparently this old guy Hue and Lucas met at a coffee shop once a week to talk about life and death. Like a mini version of the circle. They questioned the guy and he said he didn't know where Lucas went."

"Was that Hue who dropped Lucas off at the circle a while back? Dude with the cane?"

"Maybe. Must be."

"So where did Lucas go?"

"He went everywhere. One place at a time. You saw all the stuff in his room. And get this. After five years, they declared him dead. They even held a memorial service for him. They bought him a tombstone at Oakwood Cemetery. That's probably why he's so obsessed with the graveyard."

"You're making this up."

"I swear I'm not!"

"How long was he gone?"

Malik let the suspense build.

"Seven years."

"*Seven years*?!?"

"Yep. And he didn't write home once. No phone calls. Nothing. An old classmate saw him on a bridge in Prague and brought the news back to his folks, but they didn't believe it. He got some kind of GED diploma while he was in Australia. The school shipped the diploma to his parents, and that's when they figured maybe he was still alive. And then one day Lucas came back on a Greyhound bus and said he was ready to be home. That was this past summer. He called up Gideon and asked if he needed an extra hand investing in the lives of the students. Gideon was short on leaders and had known Lucas back in the day, so he let him lead a group. Supposedly, Gideon had bailed Lucas out of jail once for jumping trains when Lucas was in high school. And the rest is history."

Wayne crammed another taco into his mouth.

"We should go," he said. "I don't see the big deal. The guy took a little trip to clear his head."

We walked out to my truck without saying much. Me and Wayne sat up front. I fired up the truck and stayed in park, looking out the front windshield at the empty road.

The words he had written in the margins of the Emerson book flooded over me. Everything suddenly made sense. *I must leave in order to avoid the mediocrity that infects the masses . . . How am I standing in my own way? . . . The horizon is waiting, calling . . . If you love her, you must leave her . . . You cannot bring him back, but you can determine the future . . .*

But . . .

How could someone just leave the people they love? How could you commit so fully to yourself at the expense of others? And what was out there that was so much better than what he already had at home? Did he ever forgive himself? Wayne reached over and shifted my truck into drive.

"Brain freeze?"

"Yeah."

"Put your fingers in your ears and say 'I'm a dork.' That works."

"Seven years, man. That's a long time," I said.

29

When we got to the party, we had to park almost half a mile away because of the crowds. Word spread to all the other schools in town. James jumped out of the back of the truck and walked in the opposite direction of the party, his hands stuffed into his denim jacket pockets.

"Where you going?"

"I don't know yet," James said. "Don't feel like partying."

"What about a ride home?"

"I'll figure something out."

"Want company?"

"I'm good. Y'all have fun."

Ever since the big fight, James avoided get-togethers of all kinds. I didn't blame him. He still lived in no man's land, with us being his only friends. Our old football crew abandoned him. Everybody else in school still considered him an arrogant prick. That wasn't true anymore, but changing other people's opinions is the task of a lifetime and quite honestly not worth the effort in most cases. James wandered off into the dark streets. We knew better than to try and convince him to join us.

Cameron's dad was passed out in a lawn chair in the front

yard. I guess that counted as a chaperone. As we passed by, he abruptly grunted, "Welcome to the jungle!"

That's when I knew it'd be a crazy night. I just didn't know what kind of crazy.

Noa jumped into my arms as soon as we walked in the house. She planted a kiss on my cheek.

"Hey, handsome."

"Hey, girl."

"This is wild."

"I see that."

The house was packed with people. Half of them I didn't recognize. Music thumped against the walls and everyone shouted to hear each other. Through the back windows I could see the swimming pool filled with strangers in bathing suits and in their underwear.

"Ping-pong!" Wayne hollered. He cut through the crowd toward an empty ping-pong table. The other guys followed him.

I felt Noa's lips graze against my ear. "Hey, Colt. Can we go talk somewhere quiet?"

"Definitely."

She took my hand and led me up a winding staircase. A few of the bedroom doors were locked but we found one room that was open. Cameron must have had a little sister because the bedspread was all sparkles and she had a framed photograph of a unicorn family. We couldn't find the light switch, so Noa turned on the bedside lamp. She sat on the bed and I took a seat next to her. I waited on her to say something, and when she didn't I kissed her. Her lips tasted like the champagne lip gloss she always wore. She put her hand on my chest to keep me at bay.

"So, I really do want to tell you something."

I kissed her again and she smiled, pushing me back.

"I'm serious."

"Okay. What is it?"

"Well, I've been thinking about you. And about us, and this year, and all we've been through together. So don't freak out or anything, but I have something I want to say. I know college is going to be complicated, or whatever. And that you don't know what you're even going to do yet, even though graduation is like, right here. This is in no way meant to put pressure on you for anything."

"What are you trying to tell me?"

She took a deep breath.

"That I love you."

Now, I've smoked dope and jumped off a pier into the cold waters of the Pacific Ocean. I've kissed good-looking girls and earned straight As. I've knocked a quarterback out of a playoff game and caught a trophy bass. I've tasted five-star food and met Troy Aikman. But nothing matched up to hearing her say those words. *Nothing*. And it wasn't even close. I felt like a doctor pinned me down and put those metal shockers on my chest. All of a sudden I was full of electricity. I could have flown to the moon.

"I said I love you," she said. I could tell she was nervous because I was just sitting there like a stump.

"I love you too."

"Really?"

"Yeah, really. I do."

She kissed me.

"And, listen, about the college stuff . . ."

She kissed me again.

"I really don't know what to do about . . ."

She kissed me again and said to shut up already about college. I happily shut up and we made out on the sparkle bed for a while until someone kicked open the door and blew an air horn at us. They ran off giggling and air-horned the couple in the next room. Noa stood up and pulled me off the bed.

"Come on. Let's go hang out with everyone."

"You're torturing me."

"Well, ask yourself if I'm worth being tortured over."

I smiled.

Then everything fell apart. But I'll get there.

Downstairs, I held her hand as we moved through the rowdy masses. They had stacked all the living room furniture into a corner. Cameron's dad must have rallied because he was trying to break dance in the middle of a circle. He picked up too much speed and slammed his head into the fireplace. The circle of people dispersed and left him there bleeding into his hands. Somebody changed the song, and everyone went on with their business. Mrs. Wakefield, dressed in a ruffled evening gown, sat alone at the kitchen table drinking chardonnay and laughing hysterically at her husband's misfortune. We made our way over to the ping-pong table and found the guys mingled up with a crew of girls I didn't immediately recognize. Wayne sat on the table with a brunette standing between his legs. And then I saw their faces.

It was Jacy, the lawnmower girl.

Then I saw the rest of them.

Including Tiffany.

Yeah. *That* Tiffany. The bean queen.

Wearing a white tank top and no bra, she strolled over and kissed me on the lips.

"Hey, baby," she said. "You never called."

I pushed her away. I could feel Noa's heat rising next to me.

"Whoa. What are you doing?" I said.

"Colt, it's me. Tiffany."

"Uh, I think you have the wrong person. Come on, Noa. Let's go."

"Wait. What's going on?" Noa asked.

"Oh," Tiffany said. "This must be your unofficial girlfriend. Am I right?"

"I'm sorry. I don't know who you are or what you're talking about."

"Colt. It's me. The girl you freaking kissed on the campout?"

In retrospect, I screwed up.

Big time.

I screwed up that night we camped by letting Tiffany come too close, and I screwed up by not telling Noa about the kiss.

And I really screwed up by announcing that I didn't remember Tiffany. If you see a can of beans blow up on a person, and then that person proceeds to lose their mind and scream curse words at you while crying, you're going to remember. Everyone remembered Tiffany. She was a living legend in Wayne's book of lore.

Wayne and the others had all gathered around by now. Wayne tried to pull Tiffany away but she hissed at him to screw off or she would claw his eyes out.

"Colt . . . what is she talking about?"

I turned to Noa as a tear fell off her chin. She wiped the streak from her face.

"Oh, sweetie," Tiffany said with pouted lips. "I feel so bad now."

Noa backed away from me.

"What is she saying, Colt? Did you seriously kiss her while we were together?"

"Listen, Noa. It's . . . not what it sounds like. They came out while we were camping one night and she kissed me out of nowhere. I swear. I pushed her away. She's freaking crazy, Noa. She was covered with beans and went berserk."

"It's true!" Wayne said. "She belongs in a mental asylum!"

"Shutup! Shut your mouth!" Tiffany shrieked.

Noa backed away from me, her eyes full of hurt.

"Okay. Forget everything I said. Forget it."

"Noa . . ."

Noa pushed through the crowd toward the front door. She was gone.

30

Presley showed up to the circle wearing a white cutoff shirt and blue jeans.

He was ghostly pale. None of us had seen him wear anything but black for the last few years. He also had tattoos on his shoulders and back, which we inspected with great curiosity. He told a story for each one. His best friend lived in Port Aransas and worked in a tattoo parlor that doubled as a bait shop. Most of his choices included skulls and people being tortured by hooks and chains.

"I've heard about this group," Presley said. "There's all kinds of rumors going around."

"Yeah, well, who cares?" Wayne said.

Presley pointed at James. "Your friends seem to care a whole lot."

"Big deal. Let them say whatever they want," James said.

"That's what I said. Big deal. Everyone can only see this far in front of their face."

"How far can you see?" Lucas asked.

Presley inspected the group to make sure we weren't all playing some elaborate prank on him.

"I see eternity. All of it, all the time," he said.

Right out of the gates we found out Presley had a million ideas about religion and spirituality. He had read the Koran, the Torah, the Vedas, and other books I'd never heard about. He knew the Bible better than all of us put together. The heavy metal music he listened to was made by a group of Christian bands called the Blood Alliance. None of us believed him until he blared the music from his car and told us the lyrics were about slaughtering lambs and living sacrifices and blood on the altar. The images were gruesome, but the metaphors all added up.

"Harold told me you spit on him and punched the walls."

"Harold will say anything to get attention. He's a world-class liar."

"Yeah," I said. "He is."

"I figured you worshiped the devil or something," Charlie said.

"Why? Because I wear black?"

"Yeah."

"Well that doesn't make much sense."

"I guess not, now that I think about it."

Our group had grown to twelve members: me, Wayne, Ortiz, Charlie, Amado, Malik, James, Nate, Santino, and now Presley. The golf captain, Zeb Shaw, and the Korean exchange student, Sang, who had been living at Zeb's house all year had started showing up the previous week—both invited by James. For the last few weeks we had been discussing the word impact. When it came down to it, everybody wanted to make an impact on the world. Some people wanted to be famous and others rich and others spend a decade adventuring, but in the end all we really wanted was to live a life that impacted others and built up a legacy. But what did that mean? And what kind of impact did we want to make? No little kid climbs up to the top of a tree and gets pumped up about the day they sit behind a computer for eight straight hours a day in exchange for a hundred thousand bucks. We decided that the only way to make an impact was to offer our lives to a purpose greater than our own ambitions. That made enough sense.

Lucas read aloud.

"I went to the woods because I wanted to live deliberately. I wanted to live deep and suck out all the marrow of life . . . to put to rout all that was not life; and not, when I came to die, discover that I had not lived."

I drifted into my own thoughts. Ever since the party, I felt like I was carrying around a backpack full of rocks. I tried to call Noa over and over but she wouldn't answer. I called the home line, and her dad told me she needed some time. I wanted to be the kind of man she deserved, but quite honestly, I had a mountain to climb. I wrote a love letter and put it in her mailbox. This is what it said:

Noa,

I hate that I hurt you because you deserve all the good things in the world, and I brought you something terrible. That girl from the party doesn't mean anything to me, and I knew right off the bat she was crazy. She kissed me but I SWEAR I pushed her away and said I had a girlfriend. It's true. But she followed me around all night, then Wayne blew up the beans all over her. Then they left. I understand why you don't want to talk to me because I didn't tell you they came out there or about what she did. We didn't know they were coming, but I still could have told you and I didn't. I'm really sorry and I hate the way I feel right now because all of a sudden my life isn't what it used to be. I said I love you at the party and I meant it. I still do. Wherever I go, I want you to be there too.

I drove by a few hours later on my way to the circle, and the mailbox was empty, so *someone* found the letter.

The second thing weighing on me was what I had heard about Lucas. He talked about living to impact others, but, according to Malik, Lucas abandoned his family and let them think he died. He even had a tombstone with his name on it, for crying out loud. What did he intend for us? Why did he feel the need to influence the lives of young men? Did he want all of us to go crazy and leave our families? Was all of this some kind of self-therapy to make himself feel better about what happened?

"What do you think, Colt?" Lucas asked.

"Huh?"

I glanced up. The other guys had been reading passages from their journals.

"You have anything you want to share tonight?"

All of a sudden, I wanted to end the games. Time was running out. In a few short months all of this would be over, and what then? We'd been going around and around for a year and still hardly knew anything about this guy. I couldn't put my finger on the reason why, but I felt a strength in my hands that needed release. I couldn't go on like this for a second longer. If he expected us to keep listening to him, he needed to give us a reason. A clear one.

"I want to know what's most important in this life," I said, staring him down. "Why we're here. I want to hear it from you."

"What do you think?"

"No. Not what I think. I asked you the question."

"What's most important for me may not be important for you. That's something you need to find out for yourself," Lucas said.

"Shut up, man. Just shut up."

The circle fell dead silent.

"How come you have to be so slippery all the time?" I demanded. "I ask a question and you can't answer, even though you want all of us to spill our guts every second."

"Easy, Colt," Wayne said.

"When we set out on this journey, I told you that I was merely the conductor of the flame," Lucas said calmly. "My job is to encourage you to ask the questions, not to give you the answers."

"How come you get to decide that?"

"Would you rather me tell you what to think?"

"Well maybe we need someone to give us answers every once in a while. Plus, you give us questions and tell us what to write about in our journals, but we don't know one thing about you. Not one thing. You keep your life a secret from us, like we don't deserve to know you. I want to know something real about you."

"Yeah," Malik echoed. "Something real."

We all looked to Lucas for an answer. He took his time and added a log to the fire.

He spoke quietly, as if speaking to himself in another lifetime.

"I decided a long time ago that I had no responsibility to the expectations that others put on my life. Life is too short. It can end too quickly. In a heartbeat. You go to school, and then pay to go to more school, and get a job to pay off the debt you acquired going to school, then you settle down and do the same thing every day for the next fifty years until you die in some nursing home with your family dreading every visit. *The mass of men lead lives of quiet desperation.* But I decided not to be a part of the mass. You ask what's important to me and you want me to give some canned answer like faith or morality. But that would all be a lie. What's important to me is the truth. And encouraging you guys to ask questions about your existence, about how you're going to choose to spend your one wild, precious life, is how I can make the most impact here, right now. I don't have all the answers. I'm not going to pretend like I do. But I do know this: all of you have been gifted with breath not for selfish gain, but to do something meaningful—even remarkable—with your lives. To give more life away to others than you take. To invite others into the mystery. That's what's most important to me. Spending my short moments of life pouring myself into others."

I felt like a jerk.

"We're done for tonight, fellas," Lucas said with nod. "Go home and write about your impact. I'll see you next week."

Everyone packed up and drove off. But I sat on the tailgate of my truck in contemplation. After a few minutes, only me and Lucas remained.

"What was that about?" he asked.

"I'm sorry. Things are screwed up. The year's almost over and I don't know what I'm doing anymore."

"Tomorrow night. Meet me at the graveyard."

31

I found the iron front gates locked, so I jumped the fence. I knew Lucas was inside because I saw his truck parked down the street. He had told me to meet him at the empty field, under the tree where he gave us the swords. As I walked under the canopy of oaks, I noticed the figure of an old man moving toward me.

He walked with a cane.

I thought about turning and making a run for my car. The figure raised a hand to show he meant no harm. I stood on the side of the road and waited for him to pass. When he came close enough, I could tell it was the same guy who had dropped off Lucas at the circle months before.

"Good evening, Colt," he said. He wore a collared Oxford shirt tucked into khaki pants. "You may not know who I —"

"You're Dr. Hue Schrader."

He grinned, the wrinkles around his eyes more visible.

"It sounds like you know a little about me, already. Well, I know a little about you as well, and all the boys. And if you're as clever as I suspect, you've probably discovered a few things about Lucas by now."

I didn't say a word. Hue nodded and gently twisted his

cane into the soil.

"You know, Colt, he's a good man. Lucas, I mean. I can tell by your face that you aren't sure if that's true. You aren't sure about any of this. But I assure you that you are on the right path."

There were so many questions I wanted to ask, but I held back.

"You're lucky," Hue said. "You and the others. Not everyone gets a chance to explore as you've done this year. Very few young men are invited into something like this."

I glanced around at the maze of graves.

"Lucas is at the empty field. He's waiting on you." Hue brushed past me into the shadows. "Carpe diem, Colt."

I tried to keep an eye on him, but he vanished around the back of one of the great century oaks that shrouded the main drive.

I found Lucas sitting under the tree where he gave us our swords. He picked up an acorn and handed it to me.

"Feel this in your hands," he said. "Just for a moment."

I sat down next to him. Moonlight spread on the empty field that would one day be covered in gravestones. I squeezed the acorn. I thought about the first time Lucas had taken us here. Life had certainly changed since then. For the better or the worse was still up for debate. Since meeting him, I had lost all my friends, found new friends, got a girlfriend, lost a girlfriend, and basically realized death was hunting me down like a hungry wolf. Lucas might as well have been a ticking clock, always reminding you that your time was coming to an end and you had better make the most of it. Not everybody wants to think about death and legacy all the time. Sometimes, you just want to be normal. The average dummy wants to watch the Cowboys win another Super Bowl and make more money next year than he's making this year. Maybe that's the key to life, anyway. Living a life of quiet desperation. At least you accept reality, that way.

"Wayne told me about you and Noa. I'm sorry. I know she was special to you."

"It's not over yet."

I looked up at the sky, then down at the ground.

"It's just that—well—Wayne invited these girls out to camp with us one night and one of them kissed me. Anyways the girl went to sleep and Wayne put a can of beans in the fire and it blew up all over her."

Lucas's laugh echoed across the graveyard.

"You're joking."

"I wish I was."

"You guys are hilarious. You're lucky, you know."

"What do you mean?"

"When I was in high school, I didn't have anything like you guys have. I had a best friend, but he—" Lucas paused, and I could sense him trying to decide how much to reveal. "He's not around anymore. But he was a true friend, and we talked about real stuff. I had a girlfriend in high school, too. I'd even say she was the love of my life." Lucas grinned. He picked up a rock and tossed it into the distance. "Life is funny that way."

Right then, we heard footsteps somewhere nearby in the darkness. We turned and saw Hue wandering through the graves with his head down, reading the tombstones.

"I just met Hue," I said. "I remember him from that night he dropped you off at the circle."

Lucas nodded.

"Who is he?"

"A friend. A mentor. When I was your age, Hue took the time to sit down and guide me through my questions. I was offered all the same old answers from preachers and soul-suckers and everyone else, but Hue offered me something authentic. Something true. He gave me a place to ask questions and share my own thoughts. It changed my life, Colt."

"He kind of creeped me out back there."

"He's harmless, I promise. He teaches literature on campus. He's the reason I wanted to invest in a group of young guys. When I thought about everything he did for me, I wanted to pass that on to someone else. And one day, I hope you guys do the same. We all need people who encourage us." Lucas lit his pipe. "Can I tell you what I see in you, Colt?"

"Yeah."

"You're on the edge of rebirth, but you're unwilling to die."

I was seriously getting sick of all this coded language. Why couldn't he just tell me exactly what to do?

"I don't know what that means. Half the stuff you say, I don't know what it means."

"You're too afraid of what is waiting on the other side. You're a man caught in between."

"So, what, I should drive off in the middle of the night and leave everyone behind?"

"No."

"You did."

I took the Emerson book from my back pocket and handed it to him. He ran his hand over the cover as if it were a relic from another lifetime.

As he thumbed through the pages, his eyes lit up with memories. If Malik's story was true, some of them were painful. The notes he had left behind in the margins were like a roadmap of all the pain he had suffered, and how he planned to overcome it. After questioning the meaning of his life and facing the guilt of what happened, he had made a drastic decision. He started over, and didn't wait for permission to do so.

"That one is true, isn't it?"

"You can't be reborn unless you're willing to die," he said. "And the road to death is sometimes long. And oftentimes you have to walk it alone."

"How could you do that, man? Honestly. To leave your friends and family like that? I know what happened. I mean . . . the accident and all. But seven years is a long time."

He handed the book back to me.

"Let's stand and walk. You still have the acorn?"

I opened my hand and showed it to him. We stood and walked slowly among the tombstones. Above, patchwork clouds separated for just long enough for the moon to shine down on us.

"I wanted to make something out of my short hours, especially after seeing how quickly it could all come to an end. I couldn't live with myself for a long time. I wasn't in a healthy place. I was pretty messed up. It was my fault, Colt. I was the one who convinced him to come with me that night, and I was the one behind the wheel. He was my best friend in the world. He died because of me. I still think about him every day, the life he left behind, and the life still in front of me. I swore to live enough life for the both of us. After the accident, I lay in bed every night watching the ceiling fan go around and around until I fell asleep. Sometimes I stayed awake all night. And then one night, I had this overwhelming feeling that if I didn't do something at that exact moment, something drastic, my life would never be my own. I kept asking myself what would happen if I died in a year? Or in a week? I knew I couldn't wait any longer. So I stood up, put on my shoes, and left."

"Where'd you go?"

"That night I hitchhiked to Austin, and from there I went everywhere you can imagine. Places I can't even remember. I chased life across a thousand borders."

"But what about your family? Your friends?"

"I'm better for my family and friends now than I was then. But I couldn't explain that. For the next five decades, God-willing, I will be a better man because of the journey I took. A better son. A better father, one day. A better husband. Don't get me wrong—I made plenty of mistakes along the way that I regret. I was young and dumb. And you can say it was selfish of me to leave. Everyone did. They blamed me. They blamed Hue for filling my mind with unrealistic dreams. And it certainly created pain in my life and in the lives of others. But I had to forgive myself. That journey made my river deeper than it was ever going to be if I played it safe. And I'm able to give more of myself now than I would have been otherwise."

"Did you ever connect with the girl again? The one from high school?"

He shook his head no.

"I loved her. She loved me too. But I was gone for too long. She eventually married another guy we went to school with. I heard they have a son."

Lucas bent down and dug into the earth. He created a small hole.

"Give me that acorn."

I handed it to him and he buried it.

"One day this acorn is going to be reborn into something

great. Something completely new, that feeds the lives of others. But first it's going to suffer. Break apart. Open up to the mysteries and complexity of creation. If you dig in this ground a hundred years from now, I guarantee you won't find an acorn that has made slight adjustments to its character. You'll find roots. Transformation. There's greatness in you, Colt. Do you accept that as true?"

"I do."

"Then be great."

I looked down and saw we were standing above the tombstone etched with the name 'Lucas Raymond Oliver.'

But here he stood, alive.

32

With a month to go before graduation, I found myself date-less on prom night.

My mom assumed me and Noa were still together and she cried at the dinner table when I confessed we broke up.

"Colt . . . she was your best shot," she said, her head in her hands. "She was your best shot, and you ruined it."

I didn't know what she meant by that. When pressed for an explanation of what went wrong, I said we got our stories mixed up about something silly and decided to take a break. This idea of a short break appeased my mom, but she also started planning a rescue mission to win Noa back to our family.

Most of the guys in our group had dates. Even Peter was going to the prom, asked by Kate Lucroy after she saw him holding the door open for girls at the church. She and a couple of friends wrote 'Prom with Kate?' on the front windshield of his mom's minivan. This message was a significant improvement from the last time Peter's minivan was tagged with boners and curse words. He didn't know anyone named Kate but still said yes without seeing her picture or anything.

Everyone else found a date, too, except for me and Wayne

and James. I only wanted one girl, but, according to my mom, I had missed my shot. From what I understood, Noa turned down five or six other guys, saying she was possibly going out of town that night for a family reunion and couldn't commit. Other intel told me she planned to go to the prom with a group of girls and have a Disney movie marathon afterwards.

I parked in front of Wayne's house. His dad met me on the lawn. He wore nothing but a fishnet cap and a pair of boxer briefs.

"Hey there, Colt. I bet you're a . . . 40 long. Skinny rascal, aren't you? I thought you played linebacker."

"I was undersized."

"Hell yeah you were. Hey, though. Doesn't matter the size of the dog in the fight but the fight in the dog! I played ball in high school too. Wide receiver. Fast as a whitetail deer but our quarterback couldn't throw from me to you. It was all political, you know? Dude was banging the principal."

"Uh-huh."

"Well come inside and get yourself dressed. I cooked supper, too."

He motioned for me to follow him into the trailer but I didn't know what he meant. Me and Wayne had already decided not to go to the prom.

"What are you talking about, get dressed?"

Burt stopped at the door.

"You don't know?"

Just then Wayne walked outside in a hand-me-down, bright blue tuxedo with gold fringe on the shoulders and a gold line running down the outside of the pants. He looked like a waiter on a cruise ship in 1975.

"What are you wearing?"

"Come inside and get ready. We're going to be late."

"No, Wayne. No. No. No. We're going camping."

"Not anymore. I called James and canceled."

"I don't want to go to the prom."

"I knew you would say that. But listen, Colt. Just listen for one second. Noa might be there and you can win her back. Let's say she's sitting there at a table all alone, crying in despair. She's beautiful. Heartbroken. Vulnerable. And a slow song comes on and everybody starts dancing and she lifts her chin, tears on her cheeks, and there you are standing under the spotlight with your hand held out like this. You're telling me she's just going to sit there and keep on crying? You're crazy. This is your shot, Colt! Tonight we get her back!"

I took a deep breath. Wayne leaned against the porch and lit his pipe.

"First, I don't think she's going. And even if she does, I don't think that plan will work."

"You can't win if you don't play. It's *impossible* if you don't show up. Listen, Colt. I feel bad about the whole breakup thing. I'm carrying the blame on my shoulders since I'm the one who asked those girls to come camping with us. I should have known better. So it's my job to get y'all back together."

"Wayne . . . "

"Give me ten bucks and I can hand it to the DJ for a song. And then I find the spotlight, I put it on you, and it's easy. They'll name you the Prom King and Queen, for God's sakes."

"Slow down. We don't have tickets. They cost twenty bucks each. I don't have twenty bucks."

Burt snickered. He nudged Wayne, who also laughed.

"We'll just walk right through the doors and no one will

stop us. You act like you got somewhere to go, and there you are."

"This is all the clothes I have. And a flannel shirt in my car."

"We'll get you tailored up. There's three or four other sizes just like this one."

It turned out that several decades earlier Burt bought a convertible and found a dozen matching suits in the trunk.

The suits were spread out on Wayne's bed.

"I don't want to match you," I said.

"Are you crazy? We'll look like movie stars. They're blue tuxedos and it will be dark. No one will pay any attention to that. Plus I'll be behind the scenes, manning the spotlight."

We sat at the dinner table in matching tuxedos, eating a bowl of deli ham and beans. While we ate, Burt told us a few stories from his own high school prom, which ended with him passed out naked under the bleachers.

"I'm proud of you boys," he said. "Y'all are damn good kids. Sweethearts. Come here and let me take a photograph for your mommas."

He snapped a photo of us standing on the porch and wiped a tear. The tuxedos smelled like mothballs, so we doused ourselves with a bottle of Burt's cologne that burned our skin. That, paired with the ham and beans, made for a pungent ride to the prom. We rolled the windows down and hoped to air out before we arrived and spoke to anyone face to face.

"I want to tell you something," Wayne said after a while.

"What?"

"I'm alive because of you." He leaned his head out the window. "If you didn't invite me to the circle, my whole life would be different. I'd be driving real slow, pal. Real slow for ninety years until I lay there curled up on a hospital bed hacking my organs up one by one. Now, there's no chance in hell of me living to ninety. None. I don't know how exactly it would go, but it wouldn't be going like this. That's certain as the sunrise. That day in the parking lot was a fulcrum."

"I don't know what a fulcrum is."

"It's a turning point. I learned that word from Villarreal, of all people. After the fight. It's the pivot. Everything swings on the fulcrum. You look at the center of a clock, and the two hands are anchored at the fulcrum. And my time has come."

"What do you mean, your time has come?"

"I mean it's time. All the waiting around is over. I'm headed into the unknown. The fullness of time has arrived."

He winked at me and cranked up the Mexican music on the stereo. I turned it back down.

"What?"

"Hey. That's my favorite part. When the girl singer comes in and they get all erotic with oohs and ahhs."

"What are you talking about?"

He grinned.

"Can you keep a secret?"

"I guess."

"I need a firm yes or no."

"Yes."

"I'm out of here, pal. I'm gone like the wind. It's been decided."

"Where to?"

"Mexico first. But I'm going, going, going to the ends of the earth. Just like Lucas. The school counselor told me to make a five-year plan, and *this is it*."

"He basically ruined his whole family. You know that, right?"

"No, he didn't. He's back here now and it's like he was

never even gone. The only difference is that now he has all those experiences. Now he can go around helping other people to open their eyes up for the first time. That's the only difference. Everybody else spent the last few years picking their butts and talking about the weather. They bought border collies and opened Christmas presents once a year. Who gives a damn? I've thought about this a million ways, Colt. You gotta hear me. Time moves so fast that if we blink we're already five years down the road."

"Okay . . ."

"So if that's true, you blink, I'm gone for five years gathering up all these experiences, you open your eyes and I'm home. What's wrong with that?"

"Nothing, I guess."

"Nothing! That's right, pal. Nothing at all! And look at me. I want you to go with me. Really. The two of us. We'll be Lewis and Clark. Butch and Sundance. Colt and Wayne."

"You're serious?"

"Of course I am."

"When are you going?"

"I can't tell you. Unless you go with me."

"I think you're nuts."

"I think you're exactly right."

He shrugged and drove faster into the hot darkness.

33

Wayne blared his Mexican music as we cruised into the parking lot and found a spot near the back. We stepped out of the car in our matching tuxedos, Wayne determined to reunite me and Noa.

A line formed to the entrance where a few of the teachers confiscated the tickets. Mostly, they made sure no one was too drunk to be allowed inside. A police officer stood next to them with his thumbs hooked onto his utility belt.

Wayne skipped to the front of the line and I followed. We heard someone shout an insult about our matching suits but deterring Wayne from his mission would take a natural disaster. He gripped my arm and we walked past the teachers without a word.

Just as he suspected, no one stopped us. They probably thought we were part of an entertainment act.

Wayne put his arm around my neck and led me through the crowd of dancers. Rap music blared and a few people basically humped each other on the dance floor. What a world. What a time to be alive.

"I'm going to get some punch," Wayne said. "Operation

Noa officially begins when I get back. I'll meet you behind the stage."

I pushed through the crowd toward the stage wishing we hadn't come. Seriously, what was there to gain? I already knew that Noa was done. She was done. I saw the look in her eyes at the party. No one comes back from that. Not to mention, we were only a few weeks away from graduation and our paths were obviously going in different directions. If she needed a reason to cut the cord and move on with the next chapter in her life, I gave her one. Or, Tiffany gave her one. Maybe I just had to learn to be okay with it.

The music thudded into my chest as I moved closer to the speakers, and then it faded as I moved past them. I sat on the back wing of the stage where no one could see me.

Except . . .

Noa was there too.

Sitting against the wall, scrolling on her phone. I almost didn't recognize her because she wasn't wearing glasses. She was barefoot, her heels lying on the ground a few feet away like she had tossed them. Her hair was down and sort of curled, which I'd never seen before.

She was so beautiful.

I'm not sure how long I'd been staring when she glanced up and noticed me. She put the phone down and sat up straight.

"Hey," I said.

"Hey."

"The party's out there."

"Yeah, I just needed to sit down for a minute. And it's super loud."

I nodded, and we sat for a while without saying anything.

She kept her eyes on me, waiting for me to break the silence. Time spread out between us, expanding, expanding, and I couldn't do anything to slow it down. I needed something. A word. A question. A joke that could make her laugh. It's like my mind shut off, and I sat there like an idiot. She started to stand and I knew she was going to offer up some kind of excuse why she had to go.

"You look great," I said quickly, hoping to stall her. "Like, really great. I've never seen your hair like that."

"Oh. Thanks. Hey, sorry, but I should probably —"

The rap music came to a dead stop, and the crowd groaned. I leaned back to look around the speakers and saw Wayne talking earnestly with the DJ. He handed him a messy wad of cash. Wayne locked eyes with me and nodded slowly.

Then suddenly . . .

"Unchained Melody" by The Righteous Brothers filled the cafeteria. It appeared that Operation Noa was in full effect.

Noa rolled her eyes.

"What exactly are you up to?" she asked.

"Can we dance just one time? One song."

"Colt . . ."

"Please, just one song."

I slid off the stage and held out my hand. She cocked her head, and I detected the very slightest of smiles. She stepped forward into the light and the glitter around her eyes sparkled. She took my hand and I eased my arms around her waist. We moved back and forth to the music. Her cheek brushed against mine, and I was lost at sea.

And time goes by so slowly. And time can do so much . . . Are you still mine?

She backed away and made a funny face.

"You smell awful," she said. "And actually, you look awful too."

"It's a long story, but it's Wayne's fault."

"Ah, Wayne's fault," she said sarcastically. She came back in close to me. "Everything seems to be Wayne's fault."

Oh my darling, I hunger for your touch . . .

"I've been thinking about us. And about next year, and everything we've been through. And I don't know what it is. But something about me and you together just feels right. From the very beginning. It feels like we were supposed to be more than just . . . a high school girlfriend and boyfriend. I don't know. I'm not ready to just let us go."

"I'm not really sure what to think," she said. "Because this year, like, yeah it was amazing. And you were amazing. But I've been realizing lately that maybe everything isn't supposed to last forever—"

"Noa . . ."

She brushed a tear off her face.

"No. Wait. I've been thinking about us too and I'm not mad. I was so mad at you, but I'm not anymore. I don't care about the kiss. I believe what you said. I really do. We're just . . . Colt, we're eighteen years old and maybe this was just . . . a really good season of life. And we can be okay with that. We can go out in the world and do our own thing and have no regrets. I don't want us to hold each other back."

"I would regret losing you. Losing this."

"Do you remember our first date?"

"Yeah, every minute of it."

"I went home that night and lay in bed and dreamed about

marrying you. I know that sounds so incredibly stupid but I did. But ever since the party I've been thinking about how much you've changed this year. And how much I've changed. And we're just going to keep on changing. In ten years, we're going to be totally different people than we are tonight. I think . . . I think maybe we just caught each other in this perfect little window of time. But now it's closing, and it's not your fault and it's not my fault. It just is."

"Don't say that."

"Colt . . ."

"I'm in love with you. I'm always going to be in love with you no matter what happens."

She rested her head on my shoulder, and I could tell she was crying more now. She held me tighter, but she didn't say anything. She just cried.

I need your love. I need your love. God speed your love to me.

I wanted the song to play forever. It didn't. The music reached its crescendo and then faded away.

Noa lifted her head and forced a smile through the tears.

"Bye Colt."

She picked up her shoes and her phone and disappeared into the crowd.

Wayne leapt off the stage behind me.

"Well?" he demanded.

I watched the tail of Noa's dress vanish in the crowd.

"I'm going with you," I said. "When do we leave?"

34

I meant what I said to Wayne.

If Noa was truly gone from my life, I had no reason to hum-drum through four years of college for a degree I may or may not need. According to Wayne, you could be a millionaire with no ex-perience or degrees required. All signs pointed to the two of us staying broken up, no matter my intentions or best efforts.

Was it ever as good as I thought it was?

I went home that night after the prom and studied all the bus and train maps I could rummage up online. I still hadn't committed to any colleges yet, so that wouldn't be a problem. My parents would be mad, no doubt, but I planned to keep in touch. College could always come later.

The chief concern with setting out for a life on the road would be how to generate income. Wayne offered a long list of ideas, most of them illegal. When I shot down some of the dumb-er ideas, like buying dry oregano in bulk and selling it as marijua-na, he signed us up selling from a door-to-door catalog. The same company handled a thousand different products, so we could sell almost anything. They shipped him a catalog. Just like that we worked on the sales force of Seasons Choice International. No interview required. All they needed was a social security number and an address to send your check. He thought we would have the most success with fruit baskets. For lodging, we decided to sleep in tents or out under the stars. He calculated that in a year our savings would exceed a hundred thousand dollars. I knew it was all a pipe dream, but I didn't care. The dreaming was fun.

The next night at the circle, Lucas passed out rough drafts of the book of our writings.

"This is your last chance to turn in pages. I'm taking it to the printer tomorrow. If you forgot them at home, you can bring them by my house later."

Lucas had been hounding us to turn in our writings for a few weeks. Malik, Peter, James, Nate, and Santino all passed some new pages around the circle to be added to the book.

"Awesome. I can't wait to read this stuff."

Wayne brought out a thick stack of pages, maybe thirty or so, and handed them to Lucas.

"Here you go."

"What's this?"

"More writings. Stuff I haven't shared out loud."

"Nice."

"Also, my will and final testament."

We all realized he wasn't joking.

"Your will?" Amado asked. "Like, if you die, your will?"

"That's right."

"Smart," Presley said. "I should do the same. You got to be careful when you die that people don't come around sucking your blood. Like vampires."

"Huh?"

"Bingo," Wayne said. "I already told you guys that my life

is basically already over. A while back I had this dream where I was driving in a car going a hundred miles an hour . . ."

"Yeah . . . Yeah we know!"

"And that means I have one split second to do something meaningful with my life, like Lucas says. The last thing I need is some funeral director who smells like Lysol lining people up to cry over my waxy body. This is my will and testament. You're all witnesses. Once it's published, it's a legal document. You have to do exactly what it says unless you want to disrespect me in death, in which case I will come back as a ghost and haunt you and your family for seven generations."

Lucas took the pages and added them to the rest of his stack.

"Everybody ready?"

We left the fire burning in the circle and ran down the parking lot and through the trees to the highway. We crossed the bridge without being seen and ducked under our rafter as we had done dozens of times before. Since our first trip to the bridge, we filled the rafter with inspirational quotes and ideas that we all believed would last forever.

"Gather around," Lucas said. "Keep your voices down."

We crowded together under the bridge. Lucas sat on the stoop facing us.

"Look down there," he said. "This is our rafter, but there are eight more just like it on this side of the bridge. The opposite side of the bridge also has nine rafters. That makes eighteen total. What you guys have done this year started a legacy. Next year, you can invite the new senior guys to follow in your footsteps. Present them with the second rafter and encourage them to fill the empty spaces with words that are eternal, just as you've done here. But turn around. Look across the highway at the eighteenth rafter. One day, eighteen years from now, a group of young men will gather there and finish what you started. Those young men who will occupy the eighteenth rafter are being born this year. That's legacy. That's impact." He paused, then said, "I love you guys."

We heard footsteps on the slope of the bridge leading down to where we stood.

"Cops!"

"Stop!"

Gideon emerged under the rafter. He blasted a spotlight onto our faces.

"What the heck is this?" He shined the light on our graffiti-covered walls. "Lucas? You mind telling me what's going on?"

"This was all here," Wayne said. "We found it just like this. We're investigating a reported disturbance in the area."

Gideon shined his light on our list of names written clear as day on the concrete. Wayne slunk to the back of the group.

"I used to come here when I was their age," Lucas explained. "This is a sanctuary for these guys. A place to come and think."

"Under a bridge on a busy highway? That you've obviously defaced. I don't think so. Let's go. All of you. Right now."

We followed Gideon back to the parking lot and took seats on our tailgates. He paced around the barrel fire and paused at the stack of pages weighted by a rock. He picked up the top page, which by luck of the draw turned out to be a love poem written by Santino to his tennis instructor.

"*You are the secret in my loins,*
the anchor in my britches."

"What the heck is this, Santino?"

"It's my heart sp-sp-sp-sp-spilled on a page."

Gideon sat down and removed his glasses. He rubbed his forehead, clearly distraught over what to do with our group. He began reading another page. And another.

Malik pleaded with him. "I know you've never seen anything like this group but I swear it's changing our lives for the better, man. I swear!"

"Don't shut us down. Please."

"You know what?" Gideon finally said. He glanced down at Santino's poem again and started chuckling. "You're right. I've never seen or heard of anything like this."

He returned the pages to the stack.

"I've been doing this job for ten years, and I've never seen a group of senior guys write down their thoughts in journals and share them aloud," Gideon said. "I've never seen senior guys show up every single week without fail. I've never seen it, and I've been doing this a long time. Just try your best to keep me out of trouble, alright?"

He nodded at Lucas and headed back toward the church.

We whooped like Neanderthals until Gideon was well out of earshot.

35

The Monday after prom, I walked into the school and saw Villarreal corner a freshman girl who was wearing a short skirt out of dress code. I tried to sneak past but he caught me in the corner of his eye.

He let the girl go and chased me down the halls. "Colt! Colt! Wait up."

I hustled ahead to outrun him but he grabbed hold of my shoulder.

"I was saying your name."

"Oh, I didn't hear you."

"Better get your ears checked. Did you see me lay the wood to that punk kid?"

I walked toward first period English. He stayed on my heels.

"Yeah, I saw."

"I guess you know it's report card day." Villarreal paused and grinned. "Always surprises on report card day. With this last round of final grades, someone always gets left behind."

I stopped in my tracks.

"What are you saying?"

"Oh, I don't know. Just that some kids skip home to mommy and daddy and showcase their straight As on the fridge. And then there's the other kids. The dummies. The dull pencils." He winked. "The do-overs."

He sauntered off whistling happily. He twirled his key ring and clacked his heels on the floor.

I rushed to catch Wayne and found his locker completely cleared out. Someone said he dumped his books and belongings into the trash can. I chased him down in front of the school. He greeted me with a crazed fire in his eyes.

"I flunked," he said. "They didn't want me to pass, so I didn't."

"You can make an appeal or something. Maybe do something for extra credit?"

"No. You're missing the point. You don't see everything yet, but you will. Soon. Remember when Presley said he could see eternity all at once, all the time? Well I know what he means. My eyes are wide open, and boy, it's wild. It's wild! I see every inch of it!"

"Where are you going?"

"Home. To pack up."

"Wayne . . ."

"We're leaving tonight. You and me. Or if you wait to graduate, then you can meet up with me in Mexico. Either way, I'm going to buy us a couple bus passes, and our first order of business when we get there is to meet some hot chicks. We're going to take them to the beach and we're going to kiss and dance and go crazy like werewolves under the moonlight. Colt, we can't be the kinds of guys who live a halfway life."

"I can't leave tonight."

"Why not? Give me one good reason."

"I haven't graduated, for one thing."

"Like I said, you can meet up with me later if you really want. But you already got your final grades. Who cares if you walk across the stage? What a dumb ceremony anyways. I tell you what. When we get on the road, I'll find you a cap and gown and we can do the whole thing. We'll mail a photo to your mom. It'll be even better."

"Wayne . . ."

He put his hands on my shoulders.

"Be awake around two or three. I'll knock on your window." He'd reached a bizarre state of enlightenment. "Colt. Beautiful, beautiful Colt. One day, many years from now, you will look back at this moment, right here, as the fulcrum."

He kissed me on the forehead and sprinted off toward his car. I stood there dumbfounded.

Soon I heard squealing tires and the faint trail of Mexican radio.

36

I lay on my bed fully dressed, using my duffel bag as a pillow. Everyone in my house went to bed around ten or eleven but I hadn't slept at all. To be perfectly honest, I hadn't yet convinced myself that I was actually going to get into the car with Wayne. Or that he was going to show up. Maybe I wasn't seeing things clearly anymore. Maybe I had never seen clearly until now. I didn't know. What kind of maniac drives off in the middle of the night and doesn't tell his parents or the girl he loves? I mean . . . what would Noa say?

I felt lost. Maybe I was scared.

Or maybe I was just a world-class idiot.

Go instead where there is no path, and leave a trail. Emerson's words echoed in my head.

We had been going on adventures all year, but this felt different. I couldn't see as much light in this decision as I could see the darkness. Wayne could only see light, and maybe that was the difference between us.

I wanted a third choice.

At dinner we talked about the new recipe my mom used for chicken enchiladas. We voiced the pros and cons and unanimously voted the old recipe as superior. I tried on my graduation cap. Mom took a photo of me standing in front of the fireplace. I watched a sitcom with my dad.

Then, just like any other night, I said goodnight and went to bed.

Two o'clock came and went. I turned off the lamp and lay perfectly still, listening for the telltale signs of Wayne. The fan spun round and round. By three I wondered if he was still coming. Part of me wished he got caught by Burt or the police or whoever patrolled reckless teenagers. Or that he chickened out at the last minute. That seemed the least likely possibility. I wanted so badly for the daylight to come, and for the two of us to sit down and talk through the plan one more time.

I heard a knock and sat up in a fog.

I must have fallen asleep. The clock said 5:43. I turned on the lamp and slung my bag over my shoulder on the way to the window.

I lifted the window but no one was there.

My dad opened the bedroom door.

"Hey, Colt. Sit down."

I don't know what he thought about me standing there in my bedroom fully dressed, wearing shoes, at 5:43 in the morning. He didn't seem to notice. I figured Wayne blew the secret somehow. Knowing him, he probably told the wrong person and word traveled through the mom network back to my household. My dad didn't seem mad, though. He looked pale.

"What's going on?"

"Come here and sit down."

I sat next to him on the bed, feeling a slight chill.

"I don't really know how to say this to you," he said, somberly.

"Are you okay? Is Mom okay?"

"Colt . . ." He put his hand on my shoulder and squeezed. "I have something to tell you."

My mind flashed to Wayne. Why hadn't he showed up yet?

"You're making me nervous."

Dad closed his eyes and took a deep breath.

"Something really terrible has happened."

"Is Wayne okay?"

My dad was confused. "Wayne?"

"Where is he?"

"I don't know. As far as I know he's at home with his dad." He paused, took a deep breath, then continued, "I don't know how to tell you this, Colt. But your friend Lucas was killed last night. It's all over the news, and—"

Time never stops moving. But sometimes it slows down enough for you to see everything clearly for just a moment. If you could live in this speed, you could live forever. The forgotten things we collect in our lives suddenly find a voice and remind us of their importance, and how they too are a part of the story we are telling day by day with the breath in our lungs and the words we speak and the movement of our hands and feet. Over there was my samurai sword leaned against the window, ready to be taken on our trip, delivered on bended knee by Lucas in a graveyard. He asked if I would fight with everything I had, and I said yes. That was a promise I had to keep. I saw the tattered copy of Emerson's *Essays* on my shelf, which I had told my teacher that I lost when it was time to turn it back in. I saw names like Rilke, Gibran, and Thoreau looking back at me, all the mentors who shaped my thoughts over the course of the year. I wished they could speak out loud to me now in a chorus of voices to remind me of the beauty I so often felt stirring in my heart, but could no longer recall. I saw everything all at once—all of eternity—in a moment, just like Wayne and Presley and all the others who saw further than me. I saw the folder given to all the tutors of how to deal with difficult kids like Harold. A photo of me and Noa wearing the go-kart helmets. The scrapbook my mom finally finished and placed on my bed with a note that read, "We're proud of you!" And the last-ditch effort I made to write down in the empty journal some of my thoughts from the year so that I could fortify my chapter in the book. These scattered artifacts of my life sang a celebration song of death, just as they had been doing all year long.

"That's not possible . . ." I must have said out loud.

"Wayne's dad called me about ten minutes ago. I turned on the TV and it's the lead story on the local news. Apparently there was an altercation in his home between a few homeless men. The news anchor said he sort of kept an open door at his house. They think these two men might have been fighting over drugs, or money or who knows what. Lucas stepped in to try and stop the situation and was stabbed. One of the other guys made a call to the police but by the time they got there . . . Colt, I am so terribly sorry. I'm so sorry. It's a tragedy. I'm just so, so sorry. I know this is . . ."

I suddenly found myself moving through the dark house, leaving the front door wide open. My feet went numb on the sidewalk. I hit the pavement and ran and ran and ran for the bridge. The cool, thin air of predawn hit me in the face as I screamed tears into the darkness. Even as I ran, I remember thinking my dad was wrong. He dreamed the death of Lucas, and I dreamed he told me about the dream. I'd wake up in the bed of a pickup truck, staring up at the stars as Lucas guided us through the light years. Of all the ways Lucas Oliver could have died while out there in the world climbing mountains, jumping out of planes, paddling down rivers, it was the knife of a man in his own home — a man he was trying to help — that was the last word of his story.

Lucas deserved better.

I came to the bridge. A car drove up to the stop sign and waited for me to move, but I couldn't feel my legs and wondered if it was me who had died. *Was it me? Was the knife in me? Why was I still alive?* The headlights blasted into my face. My thoughts were scrambled and time twisted me into a knot. The lady driving the car slowly maneuvered around me, then continued on.

I ducked under the bridge and sat in our rafter and cried.

Lightning rattled on the horizon.

Craig Cunningham

37

I lay in the bed of my truck in my driveway, staring up at the spread of stars above. I thought about Lucas, and where he was now.

How could I know? What happens to a person like that after death? What did he truly believe? After spending almost a year with him, I still didn't know. I think that was his goal. If he gave us all the answers, we'd have found ourselves thinking like him rather than thinking for ourselves. He wanted our thoughts and beliefs to be our own. That's what made him so dangerous.

Summer came back with a fury, and I savored every hint of the breeze. All of a sudden I knew death was a real character in the powerful play, not just an idea. I saw him face to face, like Wayne did when the Coyote King visited his dreams. But the closer you get to death, the more you realize he's a friend. He's like an alarm clock, with the sole intention of waking you from a long period of sleep.

I was awake.

I had been invited into the mystery, and I said yes. This was the price of admission.

Earlier that morning, I made some of the hardest phone

calls of my life.

I started with Wayne. His dad had already told him the news, and he could hardly speak. At first, he was filled with rage and wanted to take revenge on whoever stabbed Lucas. He also said something about traveling backwards in time so that Lucas's death could have been avoided. Wayne needed to get some sleep. The way he was talking made me nervous. I pointed out that if anyone on earth was ready to walk into the strangeland of death, it was Lucas. Just like when he set off to see the world, with his death, he had simply set off to see a new world, and we weren't far behind. This eased Wayne's frustrations. He called half the guys on our list, and I called the other half. We decided to hold a candlelight vigil for Lucas at the circle the next night.

I missed my mentor. I missed my friend. We still needed him. We weren't ready to face the questions on our own. At least, I didn't think so.

Footsteps approached.

I sat up and jumped off the tailgate.

It was James, coming from next door. He was carrying two baseball gloves and a ball.

"Hey, man. I figured you would be out here."

"Hey."

He tossed me a glove, and we played catch in the glow of my headlights.

"You holding up okay?"

"I don't know."

"Not me," he said. "My heart's ripped out. It should be me, or anyone else, but not him."

"I'm not sure how I'm supposed to feel, I guess."

James nodded.

"I wanted to die, Colt. I really did. I tried to die and by a miracle I lived. Lucas tried to teach us how to live and he died. He died because he opened his home to people who needed help. It's screwed up, man. It should have been me."

"You can't think like that."

"Well, I do."

We threw the ball back and forth.

"You remember that morning that we drove out to Tonkawa for the first time, and I rode up front with Lucas?" he asked.

"I remember."

"He told me something that sort of changed how I was thinking about everything. He said that I didn't survive those pills. Those pills killed me, and now I was reborn as something new. That I could Carpe Diem, seize the day, every day, and live the life I always imagined. I could become whoever I wanted. That maybe the old James was dead. And so maybe this is another death. For me. For you. For all of us. But somehow we get another chance to keep on living. That's what Lucas gave us, I guess."

"That's a hell of a thing to give guys like us."

38

By the time we showed up to the vigil, Wayne had scattered hundreds of candles around the circle. He sat on the hood of his car, flicking a lighter. I could tell he had been there for hours.

"Hey, man," I said.

Wayne walked over and gave me a tight hug. He smelled like smoke from a campfire.

"You okay?"

"Not even close."

"Yeah. Me either. I'm not sure if I believe it, to be honest. He faked his own death once and maybe he did it again. You think that's possible?"

"Not this time," I said. "I heard they already cremated his body. Doesn't seem real."

Wayne shook his head and lit his pipe.

"I still say he could have faked the whole thing."

We built up the fire and waited on the others.

With the funeral scheduled for the following morning, we all wanted to pay our respects in the place we knew Lucas best — sitting around a simple fire, sharing stories under the spread of summer stars. Some of the guys were having a harder time than others. Peter bawled during the entire vigil. Lucas was the second father figure he had lost to the randomness of death. Wayne had to hold him the whole time. Amado and Malik and most of the guys were stunned into silence. No one could believe our fearless leader was mortal, much less dead.

Without Lucas, there was no one to give us direction.

At least no one we'd care to listen to.

That's when a gold Oldsmobile pulled up.

Hue stepped out, hobbling forward on his cane.

He took out a heavy cardboard box with his free arm and carried it into the middle of the circle. He set it down on a tailgate and took out a book. On the cover was a photo of us holding our swords up to the moon.

"Now's as good a time as any to give these to you guys," he said. "This is a collection of everything you have shared in the circle this year. They were delivered this morning to Lucas's house." Hue fought back tears and held up one of the books. "I'm sure he told you, but I'm going to tell you again. Lucas was really proud of you boys. He loved you. He was proud of this book, and this circle, and everything it represents. You need to know that."

Hue passed out all of the books and took a seat next to James. I flipped through the pages and saw the familiar words—words spoken around a fire by the men who had forged each other into warrior poets. With every line, I could remember the moment when those words were first shared in the circle. A flashlight pointed down at a few thoughts scribbled into a journal. I saw the faces. The moment when your heart beats so hard that you hear it thumping in your ears, and then you share something so intimate that maybe it will destroy you or maybe it will give you eternal life.

Hue cleared his throat.

"There's something else," he said loudly. Everyone perked up. He twisted his cane into the concrete as if it were a nervous tick. "We found a letter in his desk. Instructions to be carried out after his death. A will of sorts. Death was always on his mind, more or less. But you should know that he mentioned you in his final wishes."

Hue pulled a folded piece of paper from his jacket pocket and began to read.

"I'm going to skip ahead to the part having to do with you, if that's okay. *To the young men of the Sacred Circle, I cannot express enough how much I treasure each one of you. There is greatness in you, but you must believe that is true in order for it to manifest. I invite you to go on one final adventure on my behalf. Take some of my ashes, each one of you, and carry them to the ends of the earth. Go mingle with the horizons. Embrace beauty. Feed the light. Choose whatever place calls you, and take me there. Pour me out. Carpe Diem.*"

We sat in absolute, stunned silence. Was Lucas serious when he wrote that? Was this some kind of joke? Take his ashes around the world?

Hue returned the folded letter to his pocket.

"I understand this is a lot to take in." He removed a simple clay jar and small leather pouches from the box.

"Is that him?" Wayne asked, pointing at the jar.

"No," Hue replied. "That's not him. This is just his body."

I wiped the tears from my eyes. It was time to jump. It was time for me to die, just like Lucas told me in the graveyard.

I approached the clay jar and looked into the rough, powdery substance within. The guys waited to see what I might do.

"It's not supposed to end here," I said. "He asked us if we would fight with everything we have. And each one of us said yes. Each one of us made that commitment. We all took the sword from him and said yes."

I scooped ashes into the pouch and drew it closed.

"Alaska," I said.

James grinned. He jumped off his tailgate and took a pouch.

"Morocco," he announced, and reached into the ashes.

One by one, the guys came up and took the ashes, announcing where they would take them. In the coming years, Lucas would be going everywhere from Brazil to China to Peter's grand excursion to San Antonio.

Wayne waited until everyone else had gone, then stood up. He looked into the ashes and nodded. The jar was almost empty. He picked it up and walked toward the fire.

"The circle," he said, and poured the remainder into the flames.

39

At the end of summer, I drove beneath the canopy of century oaks, the windows down.

Everything I needed for the next year was inside a duffel bag in the seat next to me — clothes, books, and the pouch of ashes. My splurge purchase was a cot so that in a pinch I wouldn't have to sleep on the ground. That, a sleeping bag, a few blankets, and my sword were in the very back. Anything else, I could buy out on the open road.

The wind rustled in the leaves of the trees overhead, easing around the tombstones scattered throughout the cemetery. I imagined the wings of the stone angels filling up with that wind and spreading wide to fly.

Life is movement and growth and resilience.

And I was alive.

This year helped me know why.

The night before, I dreamed of a campfire in the mountains, surrounded by the towering silhouettes of men. I walked up to the fire slowly, my sword in hand. After a while, one of them turned to me. It was Lucas.

"Why have you come here?" he asked.

"I want to live."

He replied, "Everything you need is already within you."

I awoke with those words at the front of my heart. My sword lay on the bed next to me. Everything I needed to know in order to live life to the fullest had already been revealed to me. I had read the words of the poets and magicians and prophets from across the centuries. And they all said the same thing. The difference between one man and the next was in his response to the truth. In the courage of obedience.

Wayne stood underneath the tree, watching as my truck crawled to a stop. He lifted his hand with a wave.

"Thanks for meeting me," I said.

"How you feeling?"

"I'm ready."

"Me too."

We walked through the tombstones and came to the one with our friend's name on it, the same tombstone that Lucas showed me just a few months prior. There was his grave, right at our feet. But he wasn't there. He'd never been there and never would be.

I pointed out the spot where I had buried the acorn.

"We'll see," he said. "Maybe one day when we're a couple of dusty old farts we'll come back here and find a tree." Wayne looked up at me. "I owe you everything, Colt. I found my life. Now it's time to start giving back. There's somebody right now who needs to be invited to the circle. I gotta be that person. I can't think of anything better to do with my life."

After the night we gathered in honor of Lucas, Wayne took me aside and said he wanted to stick around town and lead the next group of guys through the circle. He wanted them to get swords, and fill up a rafter in the bridge, and go crazy under the moonlight. Hue was going to meet with Wayne every week and help out however he could. Gideon agreed to let the circle continue on church property until the eighteenth rafter was filled.

Me and Wayne watched the sun sink beneath the horizon, then said our goodbyes.

On the way to my truck, he called out to me.

"Hey, Colt."

"Yeah?"

"If you go, you have to come back. That's part of the deal," Wayne said. "Whatever you learn out there in the world, you have to bring it home."

"I will."

He nodded at me and I got into the car.

As I drove away, I watched Wayne in the rearview mirror. He knelt in front of the tombstone and hung his head.

Lucas asked if we would live, and we made a promise that had to be kept. An oath. A commitment to the road so few are willing to take. That's a promise I would remember years later on the first day I served as the leader in a circle of senior guys, with Harold among them. I would ask those young men to walk through the graveyard and consider the stories lived before them. So that they might awaken.

Everything you need is already within you.

Everything.

So I knocked on her door and waited.

Noa answered.

"I'm coming back for you."

"What?"

"I'm leaving and I don't know when I'm going to be home,"

I said. "But when I do, I'm coming for you. You should know that."

"Colt, what are you talking about?"

"That I'm going away for a while. I don't even know where. And maybe it will be months or years, but all I know is that I love you. And I'm coming back for you."

"Okay . . ."

"That's all."

I took a deep breath, nodded, and headed back to my truck.

"Hey, Colt," she called out.

I paused and turned around. She closed the front door behind her.

"Can I come with you?"

Epilogue

There he was.

Or, at least, there was the gravestone that reminded me of his life.

A decade had come and gone like a whisper, like a breath, like a singular memory that I could no longer grasp in its entirety. What could I make of these past ten years? Since the day I hit the highway with Noa at my side, I had seen the world. I chased life across a thousand horizons, and now here I was back where it all began. Time, just like he had always told us, was dissolving. There was no use trying to slow the years down. All we can do is live each and every moment to its fullest, carpe diem.

"You were right," I said. "Time is moving. But it's also dancing."

What was I to make of that journey? What was I to make of the man I had known for less than a year of my life? The impact he made on me would last for the rest of my days. I appreciated it then. I knew it then. But I don't think I will ever fully understand the magic of the sacred circle. It was our one night in a thousand years, and we all looked up in wonder at the city of stars above us.

He made me ask what I believed in my heart of hearts, and

more importantly, what was I going to do about it?

In the years after Lucas's death, I spent many nights reflecting on the circle. I pored over the passages in the book that had been written by my band of brothers. I could recite their verses inside and out. It didn't matter that the writing was terrible. That was the last thing that mattered. What mattered is that a group of young men came together and opened their souls to one another beneath the stars. In my travels around the world, I had never encountered anything that resembled our year in the circle.

Nothing. Not even close.

But I also knew deep in my soul that young men needed what we were so lucky to have experienced. I wished I could package our year in the circle and ship it to every community on earth. How wonderful would it be if there was a place where young men could gather once a week around a campfire and be encouraged to share their hopes and fears, their victories and failures, without worry that they would be cast aside for thinking differently than they were supposed to. Lucas gave that to us. What a gift. What a treasure.

I bent down on both knees and touched the stone.

I felt a hand squeeze my shoulder. Noa stood beside me.

"You okay?" she asked.

I nodded and stood to my feet. I kissed her. She had a ring on her finger and a baby in her belly. Like I said, time was dissolving. But life was also growing more and more beautiful.

"I've never been better."

She grinned. There she was. The same girl with the green eyes who sat in front of me during English Lit. Now, she was my wife. Now, she would be the mother of our daughter. I looked back down at the stone. A leaf fluttered down and landed on the grass.

"Carpe diem," I said.

In the winds of my soul I heard an echo.

A Note from the Author

Over my lifetime, I've worked on countless creative projects. None mean more to me than this one. This story was born out of a true experience I had in my own youth that shaped my heart and gave clarity to my future. After my year in the sacred circle, I determined to be a writer and tell stories. And I determined to live a life worthy of the potential that had been given to me. Certainly, I've fallen short more times than not. But the spark that was lit that year burns eternal and keeps me anchored to the truth that life is a gift of immeasurable worth, and that the love we hold for one another stands above all. I hope this story is a reminder of that. I know it is for me. If you'd ever like to discuss the ideas or get in touch, reach out to me through craigscunningham.com. As Lucas says when he delivers the swords in the graveyard, "Go. Be courageous and true."

Craig Cunningham

November 17, 2022